D1546349

GRANNY STRIKES BACK

A SECRET AGENT GRANNY MYSTERY BOOK 3

HARPER LIN

SOMERSET COUNTY LIBRARY
BRIDGEWATER, NJ 08807

This is a work of fiction. Names, characters, organizations, places, events, and incidents are either products of the author's imagination or are used fictitiously.

GRANNY STRIKES BACK

Copyright © 2018 by Harper Lin.

All rights reserved.

No part of this book may be reproduced, or stored in a retrieval system, or transmitted in any form or by any means, electronic, mechanical, photocopying, recording, or otherwise, without express written permission of the author.

ISBN-13: 978-1987859553

ISBN-10: 1987859553

www.harperlin.com

SOMERSET COUNTY LIBRARY
BRIDGEWATER NJ 08807

ONE

Getting attacked by an assassin is not my idea of the best way to prepare for a first date.

A visit to the hair salon, putting on a nice dress, and making sure my reading glasses are in my purse so I can decipher the menu? Yes, most certainly all good things to do. I remember enough about dating etiquette to know what needs to be done, even if I haven't been on a first date for forty years.

Times have changed, of course, and I've changed too. The last time I had a date, Jimmy Carter was president and I could read a menu without any help. There was no Internet dating, I didn't have gray hair back then, and I didn't get guilty feelings every time I looked at the picture of my late husband.

But one thing I certainly do remember about dating in the 1970s was that part of the preparations certainly did not include wiping a stranger's blood off the bathroom floor.

I'm Barbara Gold. Age: 70. Height: 5'5". Eyes: blue. Hair: gray. Weight: none of your business. Specialties: Undercover surveillance, small arms, chemical weapons, Middle Eastern and Latin American politics. Current status: Retired widow and grandmother.

Addendum to current status: Realizing just how much I need the few people left in my life.

My son and his family had flown off for a week's holiday in the Bahamas, leaving me alone with my small circle of friends. I immediately felt lonely. Not that my friends are bad people. They're all quite nice and pleasant. It's just that they're all old, some considerably older than I am, and frankly most of them are quite boring. Cheerville encourages that in its citizens. Nice, pleasant, and boring.

There was one notable exception to the boredom—Octavian Perry.

I met him at a Seniors' Yoga class at the Cheerville Senior Center. He was by far the least senior of anyone at Senior's Yoga. I guessed his age at about my own although he looked younger thanks to regular exercise and a healthy lifestyle. He had a lovely full head of hair (all gray, of course) and his deepest wrinkles were smile lines. Octavian smiled a lot. It was infectious.

I was smiling already as I applied my make up, examining myself in the bathroom mirror. He was due any minute to whisk me off for dinner at the Adowa Restaurant, a new Ethiopian place. He had billed it as "wonderfully exotic."

No, Octavian, eating at a middle class immigrant's bistro in a leafy suburb isn't exotic. Grilling camel meat while taking mortar fire in the Sahara is exotic, but nice try.

I chuckled to myself, wondering how Octavian would react to a situation like that.

Just then Dandelion crawled up my leg, ruining the fifth pair of pantyhose that week. The little tortoiseshell kitten had surprisingly painful claws, especially when she decided I was something to climb on.

"Oh, do behave," I scolded her, shaking her off.

She landed on the tile and looked up at me.

"Hungry?" I asked.

She only stared. I decided not to get into a staring contest with a cat. It's like playing drinking games with a Russian. You will always lose.

"I'll feed you before I leave, and stop turning

me into a batty old lady who talks to her cat, I'm trying to recapture my youth here."

Just then Dandelion whipped around and stared out the bathroom door, eyes going wide. She bolted out the door, stared at something towards the back of the house, and shot away in the other direction.

I paused.

That had been odd, and a lifetime of training had drilled into me that odd was bad. Odd could get you killed.

Then I felt it—the faintest breeze of night air. I had already closed all the windows in anticipation of leaving for the evening, so I shouldn't be feeling that.

Unless someone had opened a window.

But I couldn't hear a thing. While my sight wasn't what it used to be and my knees were going, my hearing remained just as sharp as ever.

Whoever had just broken into my home knew how to move silently. That suggested this wasn't some clueless teen acting rebellious or some clumsy druggie desperate to steal my TV for a fix.

I glanced around my bathroom for a weapon. I had maybe five seconds to arm myself. Safety razor? I didn't have time to break it open and make a proper blade out of it. Soap dish? Good for a club but a bit small. Nail file? No good unless I hit an eye or shoved it up a nostril. I've done the nostril thing. It has an immediate and quite horrible effect on the target but requires an excellent aim and my reflexes aren't what they used to be.

Hairspray! A nice big metal can with a hard edge on the bottom. Pretty nasty to spray into the eyes too.

I grabbed it and turned on the tap in the sink.

Then I got behind the bathroom door and closed it partway. Luckily for me the door opens inward and the sink is not visible from the hallway outside. Also, the mirror was set in such a way that you couldn't see my reflection from the doorway. These little details are essential in a battlefield, and my bathroom was about to become one.

I stood there, gripping the hairspray bottle and trying to hear above the rush of the water. Of course I heard nothing, but the running tap would lead the intruder right into my little trap.

Even when he came through the door I didn't hear him. He was a blur of motion rushing into the bathroom and going for the sink. All I saw was a man clad all in black, with a balaclava covering his face and tight black leather gloves on his hands.

Just as he stopped, realizing he'd been had, I clonked him right behind the ear with the hairspray.

I brought the hard edge of the bottom of the can precisely down on a pressure point.

Even at my age I'm up for one good hit, and I sure gave it to him. Any normal adult male would be laid out on the floor unconscious.

This was not a normal adult male, and he didn't take his cue to drop out of the fight. Very discourteous.

I did have the satisfaction to see him stagger forward and grab hold of the sink with his free hand to steady himself. His other hand gripped a Bowie knife with a serrated edge.

Yes, serrated, like I was a steak or something.

When I was younger I always found being looked at by men like I was some piece of meat to be very insulting. I still didn't like it, although now it wasn't so much insulting as downright frightening.

The intruder spun around and took a swipe at me with that serrated edge. Luckily I'd stunned him enough that his aim was off and he missed me by an inch.

I didn't give him time to improve his aim. I sprayed him full in the eyes with the hairspray.

He grunted and took a step back, allowing me to exit the door first. What a gentleman!

I ran, or what passed for running these days, to my bedroom where I had something infinitely better than a can of hairspray—a 9mm automatic pistol that I kept in a drawer in the bedside table.

Within a moment I heard his heavy footsteps coming after me, running much faster than I could and no longer caring about silence. I sprayed behind my shoulder without looking as I hurried down the short hallway to my bedroom, then tossed the can behind me. It hit him in the face with a satisfying *clonk* but didn't slow him down.

The bedroom door slamming in his face was much more effective. The door and the entire doorframe shook from the impact. It brought up memories of Cliff. Cliff had been a fellow operative. Once we shared a hotel room while on assignment in Nicaragua, posing as husband and wife. Cliff decided that we should method act, so I kicked him out and told him to sleep in the hallway. When he tried to bluster back inside "his" room, I slammed the door right in his face.

Cliff had gotten the message. This guy would not.

I clicked the ridiculously weak lock shut and hurried for my gun. Just as I thought, a second later my assailant gave the door a good swift kick and it crashed open. The average American door is ridiculously weak, a downside of living in the stable country.

He strode into the bedroom, knife held high …

… and bolted out again as I pulled out my gun.

Me being a responsible gun owner saved his life. Some paranoid people leave the safety off so they can draw and fire a half second quicker. That's such an obviously stupid practice that I won't even bother explaining why one shouldn't do that.

Leveling the gun, flicking off the safety, and aiming gave him just enough time to leap back into the hallway and duck around the corner.

I was already squeezing the trigger.

The bullet punched a hole in the door to the linen closet at the other end of the hallway and not in the intruder's skull as intended.

Oh well, it was an eleven-round clip.

I moved down the hall, leading with the gun and coming around the bend fast and well away from the corner in case he wanted to grab at my weapon.

The dining room was empty. A soft sound from the kitchen to my left told me where to go next. I edged around the doorway to the kitchen, ready for a gunfight.

I didn't get one.

He was gone, out the window he had climbed in. I flicked off the light so I wouldn't make a good target and kept low as I moved to the window. Peering out, I didn't see a thing in the yard.

He'd fled. Whoever he was, he'd come carrying only a knife. Obviously he wanted to kill me quietly, and I'd upset that little plan.

I closed and locked the window and checked every other lock in the house. Not that it would do much good. This guy had moved like a professional.

A professional assassin, going after little old me?

Just then the doorbell rang.

Octavian, no doubt.

What is it with men and their timing?

TWO

"Hello, lovely lady!"

There he stood, all done up in a nice white suit, red tie, a red handkerchief in the breast pocket, and holding a bouquet of roses. A full dozen. So much more gentlemanly than my previous suitor, although I must admit my masked man had certainly gotten my pulse racing.

Octavian flashed me a grin. He was obviously proud of his teeth, which were straight and even with just enough imperfections to show they were real. Real teeth had become something of a rarity in my social circle. I certainly wouldn't slam a bedroom door in Octavian's face. I wouldn't want to wreck that smile.

I looked past him, glancing up and down the

street. No unfamiliar cars. No laser gun sights training in on me. No knife-wielding killers hiding in the bushes as far as I could see. It looked like my visitor really had left.

For now.

"Expecting someone else?" Octavian asked.

"Um, no. I thought I heard a loud bang a minute ago."

"Probably someone who doesn't know how to park hit another car or something," Octavian said, sounding uninterested.

Suddenly I remembered myself. "Oh, what beautiful flowers! Thank you!"

"Not as beautiful as you."

I giggled. Actually giggled. And I'm not the giggling sort. I must admit that he pushed all my buttons. Being a seventy-year-old widow with few friends, this kind of attention is most welcome, especially from a charmer like Octavian.

I invited him in, even though the place showed signs of a recent life and death struggle.

"Sit down, I just need to finish getting ready."

I gave him back the flowers and hurried to the bathroom, leaving him sitting in a rather bewildered state on the couch.

Closing the door behind me, I took a quick look around. The floor near the sink was spattered with blood. Good. That might make my unwanted visitor think twice about coming back.

Or not. More likely he'd come back with a firearm.

I grabbed some toilet paper and wiped it up, tucking away some of the bloodstained paper in a cabinet in case I needed DNA evidence later. Then I went back to the hall, picked up the dented can of hairspray, and took a look at my bedroom door. There was no way to hide the splintered doorframe or the foot-shaped crack in the door itself. Then there was the bullet hole in the linen closet.

Hopefully Octavian wouldn't ask to use the bathroom, otherwise I'd have some awkward explaining to do. At his age many men had to run off to the restroom fairly frequently. I was banking on Octavian's prostate being in as good condition as his teeth.

Now that my commode looked a little less like an attempted murder scene, I rejoined Octavian in the living room. He hadn't moved an inch. I took the flowers, rewarded him with a peck on the cheek (that's all you get on a first date with me), and fetched a vase to put them in.

"Aren't you going to turn the light on?" Octavian asked when I went to the kitchen sink in the dark.

"No, I don't want to make myself a target for snipers," I replied as I filled the vase with water.

"I beg your pardon?"

"Carrots. I eat lots of carrots to help my night vision. And moving around in the dark is a good exercise for the eyes. It helps the carrots do their job."

I knew I sounded like a nutcase, but I had just survived an attack and had kissed someone for the first time since James passed. My thirteen-year-old nephew Martin didn't count. Any time I kissed the boy he made pukey noises and rubbed the kiss off with his sleeve. And just two years ago *he* used to kiss *me*.

I returned to the living room, still giddy, just in time to see Octavian notice the photo of James on the mantelpiece.

To his immense credit, he did not pretend not to see it. Instead, he walked right over to it.

"So is this the luckiest man in the world?" he asked. Octavian has a way with words.

"Yes, that's James."

"I see he was a hunter. I never did much of that myself."

James and I had worked on various missions together, and I wanted to photo in my living room to remind me of that but maintain the secrecy we had sworn to uphold. So I had chosen a photo of him in simple camo without any noticeable military gear while holding a high powered rifle with a scope. He sat on a rock in a cedar forest, looking as handsome and tough as he always had. He did, indeed, look like he was on a hunting trip.

Except that he had been hunting terrorists in the Lebanon Mountains. No need to mention that to dear old Octavian.

Looking at all those the trees in that photo, Octavian probably wouldn't have believed me anyway. Most people who haven't been to the Middle East think it's all sand dunes and pyramids. There are actually green places in some parts, and the mountains and valleys between Lebanon and Syria look more like the southwest of France than something out of the *1001 Nights*. Even Saudi Arabia has some green mountains. The highest even have ski resorts. No, I'm not joking, actual ski resorts with real snow and real skiers. Of course the law requires that men go down one side of the mountain and the women, fully veiled and clad head to toe in black robes, swoosh down the other side. They look like inkblots rolling down a giant sheet of paper. Oh, the things you see in government service!

"What did he hunt?" Octavian asked.

"Big game."

Like the chief bomb maker for Hezbollah.

"I shot a couple of deer when I was younger," he looked at me askance, then added quickly. "To please my uncle. He was a big outdoorsman."

"Don't worry about me," I said. "Deer are cute, but they're tasty too."

Octavian laughed. "I can see why a big game hunter wanted to marry you. I'm surprised you don't have any of his trophies on the wall."

"They wouldn't match the decor."

Besides, Suleiman al-Hosni had been a very ugly man, and there hadn't been much left after we finished with him.

"Shall we go?" Octavian asked.

"Certainly."

Octavian bowed to the photo. "I'll have her home at a decent hour, sir."

I smiled. I still felt a bit of guilt about doing this, even though James and I had had many conversations about the need to continue with our lives if one of us didn't come back from a mission. Except we always did come back. Who would have thought that he would die of a heart attack in bed just three years into retirement? Still, I did feel a bit odd going on a date only a couple of years later.

You might think that I'd be more worried about

the assassin who had broken into my house than the eleventh-hour rebirth of my love life. But I felt pretty sure I had scared him off for the moment, and if he did decide to come back it would be best to be gone. I fully intended on calling the police as well as my contacts in the CIA, but I needed to think this through first, figure out who might have done this. James and I had a long list of enemies.

And what better way to think than to share Ethiopian cuisine with a handsome man?

THREE

We set out in Octavian's black Mercedes. He had been a stock broker before retirement, obviously a successful one.

Once we had pulled out of my street and were heading across town I felt much better. I didn't want to involve Octavian in all this, whatever "this" was, but I couldn't tell him of my secret life in order to warn him, either. Several political careers and the fate of more than one Third World nation hinges on the fact that virtually no one knows who I really am.

Yes, I know that sounds like a boast. It's not.

The Adowa Restaurant was brightly painted in red, yellow, and green. The walls sported posters of smiling natives, a spectacular waterfall, and some odd churches that were set in large pits on a rocky plain. Upon a second look I realized that instead of being built up, they had been excavated out out of the bedrock, a sort of construction in reverse.

A gorgeous young African woman with long cornrows brought us into the dining room. There was a tense moment when she directed us towards a low table covered with an ornate brass tray. There were no chairs, only cushions on the floor. They looked quite comfortable and traditional, and impossible to rise from.

Perhaps Ethiopian senior citizens have better knees than the average American.

The gal eyeballed us and moved us over to a less authentic table that actually had chairs.

Perhaps I've gotten ethnocentric in my golden years, but chairs are a darned good invention.

We settled in. The place was about a third full, mostly with couples who looked like they were on dates. I spotted only one family. The two parents were eagerly trying to get a pair of teenaged twin girls interested in their food. The girls looked identical, and had identically bored expressions on their faces. It was obvious they had no interest in enjoying a cultural experience.

My son Frederick had been like that. He didn't even like Cinco de Mayo, saying Mariachi music made his ears hurt. Taco Bell was about as ethnic as he would go. I always knew he was destined for the suburbs.

"So how was your week?" I asked to drown out a pair of identical teen voices whining in identical fashion.

Octavian let out a sigh.

"A bit dull, to be honest. I miss the club."

"I miss it too," I lied. The club he referred to was an illegal gambling den run by some mobsters. This little romance with Octavian was actually a result of my infiltrating the club in order to investigate the murder of one of its members. I was greatly relieved to discover Octavian wasn't the culprit. I found the real murderer and shut down the illegal operation at the same time, much to the detriment of my new boyfriend's social life.

The mention of the club gave me a cold, unsettled feeling in the pit of my stomach. When I busted the place, with the reluctant assistance of Cheerville's police chief, I got spotted by the mobsters' special security man, someone went by the charming street name of "the Exterminator". You could hear the capital letter in the way the mobsters said it. I didn't know what his real name was, where he was from, or any other information.

Just a fleeting glimpse from a passing car, and a rugged, soulless face sizing me up.

Could it have been the Exterminator who had broken into my house?

That seemed unlikely. The mobsters had already lost. Some had been killed and the rest had cut and run. Those who had run had gotten away. The trail had gone cold and the police had all but given up on pursuing the case.

So why would the crooks add to their troubles by committing murder? Despite all their faults, people in organized crime were rarely vindictive with police or normal citizens. It didn't pay. There was no reason to rub me out, so why would they?

But I couldn't discount the possibility that it had been the Exterminator. The timing was so close. Besides, in the five years of my retirement my cover had never been blown, and no one from my past had come back to haunt me.

"You look happy," Octavian said.

I realized I was smiling. Yes, a case always makes me happy. Some people can't retire. I'm one of them. One might think I'd be happy to leave that life behind and enjoy a well-earned rest. Not everyone can handle being attacked one minute and going on a date the next. I thrive in that sort of atmosphere.

"It's just so nice to be out and active," I replied as honestly as I could.

Octavian looked around. "Nice decor, isn't it? And the food is delicious. My son took me to an Ethiopian place in Boston. I must admit that I was dubious at first, but it's excellent food. Spicy, but flavorful spicy, not 'blow the top of your head off' spicy."

The waitress brought some water and the menu. I looked through it and saw pictures of various gloppy concoctions of different colors. Unusual names such as *doro wat* and *lega tibs* were written beside them.

"Perhaps you should order since you've been here before," I said, handing the menu to him.

Octavian sat up a little straighter. Nothing like being put in charge to bolster a man's ego.

"Do you have any dietary restrictions?" he asked.

"I'm a gluten-sensitive ovo-lacto pescatarian."

Octavian's face fell. "What on Earth does that mean?"

"I'm not sure, but it's the trendy thing nowadays, isn't it?"

"I spend time with people my own age so I don't have to follow the trendy thing."

"I got that from television. If you want to know

about video games, my grandson has taught me all sorts of interesting and useless trivia."

"I hardly watch TV any more and when I see my grandkids I take them to the park with a strict no video games rule."

"Good man. To answer your question, I don't have any allergies and I'll eat anything that won't try to eat me back."

Octavian studied the menu again. "We'll get a sampler so you can try out a bunch of things. We'll get the *doro wat*, the *shiro de kibbe*, and some vegetables. Plus my favorite, *lega tibs*. That's beef. No meal is complete without beef."

I jumped a little at that last statement. James used to say the exact same thing. A little bundle of guilt and excitement wrestled inside me. Octavian ordered and we chatted pleasantly while I tried to keep things cool. I wondered if he felt the same mixture of feelings that I did. Probably. Any time he spoke of his late wife it was with a note of adoration. They had enjoyed a good life together. His happy go lucky style these days hid what must have been a fair amount of pain. No one our age didn't feel it. We had all lost people near and dear to us by this point in our lives.

The meal was as good as Octavian promised. It came on a platter of spongy bread called *injera*, which tasted a bit like sourdough. You ate with your hands, ripping off a piece of bread and using it to grab portions of the gloppy piles arranged around the platter.

Octavian had been right; Ethiopian food offered a nice balance of spices without ever getting too hot. The *lega tibs* were a bit on the edge, but I left those mostly to the carnivore at the table. I liked the *doro wat*, a bright red chicken stew, and the *shiro de kibbe*, while a bit rich for my taste, was an equally delicious mixture of butter and chickpeas.

The best part came after. Instead of just giving you a coffee to perk you up after your meal, the Ethiopians put on a whole coffee ceremony. That young Ethiopian gal came back with a brazier that she set on the floor next to our table. She sat on a cushion next to it and roasted the beans right in front of us, wafting the rich aroma into our faces with a reed fan. Then she ground the beans and brewed the coffee. It was rich, sweet, and strong, and came with popcorn of all things. All in all, an excellent meal.

The company was good too. Octavian was quite the charmer, and could talk on any variety of subjects while still remembering to allow a lady to speak. He asked me all sorts of questions about my past and I fell into the usual cover story of being a government bureaucrat involved with international development. That explained my extensive travels without getting too close to the truth. I had told people this story so many times that I almost believed it myself. I even had a stock of completely bogus anecdotes, funny stories that never happened about people who didn't exist.

I could go on all night about my fake life. It used to be as automatic as breathing, but now I felt a slight unease that increased throughout the meal. It took me a while to realize what exactly I felt.

It felt like I was lying, not the lying that was necessary for survival in my old career, but the base deception of someone I cared about. I had felt the same way when spinning tales of my fake life to my son, his wife, and their child. While it was even more necessary to keep them in the dark about my double life in order to protect them, it had never sat well with me. They were too close to my heart for all those necessary lies not to feel like deceit, and I didn't want barriers between myself and those important to me.

So why was I feeling that way when giving alibis to Octavian?

Oh dear, could I really be falling for someone that hard, at my age?

FOUR

Arnold Grimal, Police Chief of the City of Cheerville, did not look happy to see me. The last two times I had visited him, I had upset his easy routine of issuing parking tickets and directing traffic by dumping him with nasty cases of cold-blooded murder. When I assured him there hadn't been a murder this time, he looked relieved. When I told him I had been the target of one, he looked almost smug.

Police Chief Grimal was in his middle fifties, a good 15 years younger than me, but he did not look much healthier. His paunch draped over his waist-line so much that it hid his belt. That paunch was currently being expanded with a takeaway box of sweet and sour chicken that he was actually using chopsticks to eat. I would have not been surprised if he had used his hands.

Further evidence of bad habits was written all over his face in the form of red splotches on his nose and cheeks. The sure sign of a heavy drinker, although not, as far as I had seen, on duty. Grimal may have been an underachiever, but he was not a total screw up.

Grimal's hair had gone thin on top yet retained its sandy color. Like many men going bald, he had tried to divert the eye with facial hair—in his case a thick moustache that might have been fashionable back when bellbottoms and mood rings had been popular. It only seemed to highlight his baldness. Not as bad a choice as a comb over, but a close second.

"Are you sure he was trying to kill you? He could have been a burglar," the police chief said. Even as he said it he sounded like he didn't believe it himself. Burglaries were rare in Cheerville, and I had been at the center of too much trouble for Grimal not to believe in an assassination attempt.

"He moved like a professional, and he came straight for the room I was in with a knife. He wanted to be silent, but painful. The knife had a serrated edge."

Grimal wrinkled his red nose in disgust. He did

not care for the darker side of police work, like the real crimes where people got hurt or even killed. It upset his stomach, although this time it didn't stop him from shoveling some more sweet and sour chicken down his gullet. I guess my near-death experience offered no threat to his digestion. On the desk in front of him lay a fortune cookie. I wondered what it said.

"Any idea who could have done this?" he asked as a drop of red sauce fell from his lower lip and landed on his tie. It joined stains from some yellow and brown food that had probably constituted breakfast. Soon he'd have a broad enough palette to rival Van Gogh's *Starry Night*.

"Plenty of ideas. You're not going to like my top candidate."

Grimal grunted, a simian sound that expressed that he agreed that he wouldn't like what I said next, but would believe what I said, and that would make it worse and the whole thing was going to be far more trouble than he wanted to deal with, and the worst of it all was that he had no choice about helping me and really would just prefer it if I moved to some more active precinct where they could handle my double life so he could live in peace.

Quite an eloquent grunt, really.

Nothing came after the grunt. Grimal was the kind of cop who didn't ask questions he didn't want the answers to.

"I think your old friends from the casino are back," I said.

Grimal plopped the chopsticks back in the cardboard box and glared at me. The effect was somewhat ruined by the spray of sweet and sour sauce that hit his shirt, looking oddly like a miniature shotgun blast.

"They weren't my friends," Grimal said.

I treated him to a level gaze. Since my shirt wasn't covered in Chinese food, I had a distinct advantage in the I Want To Be Taken Seriously department.

"You looked the other way because of your brother-in-law," I told him.

Said brother-in-law was Travis Clarke, the county coroner, who had been deep into debt with the mobsters and had gotten his debt forgiven by writing off a murder victim's death as suicide. With a single phone call I could take away Grimal's and Clarke's jobs, and their liberty.

And Grimal knew it.

The police chief shifted in his seat, deep in thought. That wasn't something he was accustomed to. At last he said,

"How do you know it was him?"

"I don't, just a hunch."

Grimal gave me another of his eloquent grunts. This grunt told me he didn't much care for my hunches unless I could back them up with some solid evidence. He didn't want to deal with the mobsters again. Grimal had gotten off relatively lightly and was afraid that following up any leads on the Exterminator would be like kicking a hornet's nest.

The man expressed more with his grunts than his words.

"How's the shoulder?" I asked.

Grimal had gotten shot in our previous run-in with the casino mobsters. I was hoping that mentioning that fact might revive any flickers of alpha male pride that he must have had when he had joined the police force all those years ago.

A false hope, it turned out.

He rubbed his shoulder and glanced up at the award he had received from the governor for heroism in the line of duty. Next to it was a collage of newspaper headlines praising his "fine police work" and "bravery under fire". I didn't mind his taking all the credit—he did come in and help at a critical moment, after all—but I felt I deserved some loyalty in exchange for my generosity.

"Still hurts," he muttered.

"Don't you want to get back at them?"

"We killed a bunch. We're even."

The "we" was not quite accurate, but I let it slide. I tried a different tactic.

"Need I remind you that—"

Grimal glared at me again.

"That you have the head of the CIA on speed dial and you can have my job any time you want? Yeah, I know all that," he snapped.

Finally, a bit of feistiness! Maybe there was some hope for him after all.

I reached into my purse and pulled out a ziplock bag containing the bloody toilet paper.

"When I clonked him on the head he bled on my floor. See what the lab can do with this," I told him.

He took it gingerly. "The DNA database is huge. It takes ages to get through, and if the perp hasn't been arrested in the last few years, he won't even be on it."

"I know, but it can't hurt to check it out. Run a test and see if it comes up with anything."

Grimal nodded reluctantly and put the ziplock bag in his desk drawer. I wondered if I would ever see it again. Not that it mattered much. I had only given him half of the bloody toilet paper. The rest was safe in another ziplock bag in my refrigerator. I wasn't about to trust someone like Grimal with the only evidence I had.

"But why would he come after you?" Grimal asked. "He got away, and the casino is gone. There's no money in hurting you."

I shrugged. He had a point. It didn't make sense that the Exterminator would come calling. The damage to the organization had already been done.

Unless they feared there would be more damage.

Perhaps this was bigger than we thought. Instead of simply a small, pop-up organization of a few men moving from city to city, maybe the Cheerville casino had only been one branch of a much larger organization. If that were the case, then the Exterminator, being the organization's chief of security, would want to get rid of me as a threat.

I told Grimal my idea. He thought for a moment, doubt clouding his face, and then his eyes went wide.

"They might come after me!" he said. His voice went up an octave and his words came out as a warble, never a good thing to hear coming out of a man's throat.

"They might," I replied, relishing his look of

panic. Actually I doubted they would go after him. I was the much easier target. An unknown grandmother gets killed during a break in? All too common, sadly. A recently decorated police chief gets killed during a break in? That would set off a nationwide manhunt.

No, they wanted to kill me to send a message to him.

"They might go after my family, too," he said in a tremulous whisper.

"They might," I said, and the fear that I wanted to instill in him shot through me. What if they decided to go after Frederick and Alicia? Or even my grandson Martin?

Good thing they were in the Bahamas, but they were coming back at the end of the week.

I had to get this thing solved before then.

"We need to get on this fast," Grimal said, echoing my words. He took the ziplock bag back out of his drawer. Suddenly it had become a priority.

"Check on that, and see if there are any leads on other illegal gambling operations in this state and surrounding states," I told him.

He frowned at me. "Don't tell me how to do my job."

I could have come back with something, but

decided not to. I had finally gotten him on my side for this one, so there was no need to antagonize him. I think that little gunfight he came late to had acted as a bit of a wakeup call to just how dull and unimportant his career had been. The undeserved adulation from the governor and the press must have tasted bittersweet as well, considering that breaking open the case and taking down the bad guys had mostly been my work.

I stood up. Grimal looked at me warily. I pointed to the fortune cookie.

"What does it say?" I asked.

He shrugged, cracked it open, and pulled out the slip of paper.

"You will live a long and glorious life," he read.

I burst out laughing.

"What's so funny?" he asked, growing red.

"Nothing, have a nice day," I said as I headed out the door.

"So what are you going to do?" he asked.

"I have my own leads to follow. I'll check in later." I gave him a cheerful wave and walked out.

Yes, I had an idea how I might find out if the Exterminator worked for a larger organization. Unfortunately, that meant using poor old Octavian as bait.

FIVE

It proved to be remarkably easy. I called Octavian the next day, ostensibly to thank him for a lovely dinner. After a bit of idle chit chat I mentioned how much I missed "our little club" and wished I could bet on horses again. He jumped eagerly into that line of conversation, complaining that he never got together with the old gang any more and that life felt dull without the casino around.

I resisted the urge to judge him. Everyone has their vices, and while gambling is one of the stupider ones, it's less harmful than some. Octavian was a bit too hooked on games of chance, but he knew when to say when. He hadn't gotten in debt to the mobsters who ran the old place, and he obviously wasn't hurting for cash. If he chose to waste it in that manner, who was I to judge?

Well, I did judge, but not too harshly.

"Aren't there any other clubs around?" I asked. "Surely Cheerville couldn't be the only one."

Octavian sighed. "I wish I knew. I'll ask around. I know Cynthia has been looking."

Cynthia McAlister had been one of the regulars at the old place, and for a time had been on my suspect list for a murder. She hadn't done it. In fact, the bored, sloppy housewife hadn't done much of anything with her life. I pegged her as a person who once had big dreams and let them slide after she got into married life, as if a spouse and children were any reason to give up on your aspirations. Quite the opposite. What sort of example will you set your children if you end up being a depressed couch potato who has given up on life?

"Why don't you check with Cynthia to see if she's found something?" I pressed.

"All right," Octavian said, the eagerness brightening his voice.

We were in luck. Octavian called back just a few minutes later. It turned out that Cynthia had a line on a place in Apple Bluff, a town not too far away. The stickler was that it was invitation only and she didn't have an invitation. She had only heard about it second hand.

That was good enough. We got the address and started making plans to visit.

Yes, I was using my new boyfriend as a tool to infiltrate what I suspected to be an organized crime syndicate with a professional hit man on the payroll. Not a dull moment with Barbara Gold!

And yes, I did feel bad about doing that. In my line of work I've had to use many unwitting and undeserving people as my tools, often putting them in harm's way. That was just part of the job. It was a crummy thing to do, not matter how much I talked about the greater good. I was in danger, my family was in danger, and Octavian himself could even be in danger. What if the Exterminator had spotted Octavian's Mercedes when we had driven off together? Octavian might be helping himself out as much as he was helping me.

But all those thoughts, however valid, were mere justifications. In reality I was using him because it was necessary.

That didn't sit well with me, so I decided to keep him out of it as much as possible.

The best way to do that was to go there by myself and try to keep him from going.

Making excuses for why I couldn't make it the next day, I decided to go on my own. I hoped Octavian would keep his promise of waiting to go with me.

So the next day saw me doing something I hadn't done in a very long time—putting on a disguise. I couldn't run the risk of anyone recognizing me there.

I stood in my son's bathroom—I had moved over to their place since it was safer and I had to water the plants anyway—and pulled out my old, dusty disguise kit. It came in a small suitcase and contained a variety of wigs, false beards and moustaches, hair coloring, makeup, and prosthetics. With this kit I could make myself look like anything from a middle-aged woman to an old man.

I decided not to try for being a man. I was too short to really play the part and I no longer had any male clothes that fit me. At times in the Middle East I had pretended to be a man. It brought more respect and freedom of movement. I didn't need to worry about that here. Casino owners look at their male and female customers equally. With an equal amount of contempt.

I decided to go for a woman, someone slightly younger but obviously getting on in years. That would explain my slow movements and somewhat tremulous voice.

As a first step I decided to die my hair a bright red, such a bright red that it was obviously nothing close to my real color. Thankfully the kit came with a dye that washed out with shampoo and water. I wouldn't want to be stuck with that color. To change the style, I frizzed it out as much as it would go, using up almost an entire can of hairspray. I gave my eyebrows the same coloring and caked my face with makeup. Then I put on a red blouse, red slacks, and a pair of red heels.

I would have liked to have changed my eye color with some colored contacts. The kit had a full range of them. Sadly, they had expired a few years ago. I didn't dare put them in. My eyesight is bad enough already, thank you very much.

I examined myself in the mirror. The result was dreadful. I now looked like some aging party girl desperately trying to hold onto her misspent and long-departed youth. In other words, I looked the exact opposite of the sensibly dressed, anonymous grandma I usually looked like. It pays to be unobtrusive in my profession, and that had become a habit even in civilian life. Now I was hiding in plain sight.

Hmmm … not plain enough. While the look

was convincing, my face still retained too close of a resemblance to my own. I could fool the casual viewer, but not someone experienced like the Exterminator. While I had only had a brief glance of him, I suspected he had been watching me for some time before he had made his move. He knew exactly what I looked like. A professional like him would not be fooled by this get-up for long.

I needed something more, something radical.

The disguise kit had just the thing.

I opened a little tin that contained a variety of prosthetic moles. I picked out the biggest one, which came complete with two long, black hairs sticking out of it. Adding a bit of adhesive to the bottom, I stuck it on my cheek close to my nose.

I examined my handiwork. All eyes would be on that mole. No one would remember the rest of my face.

"Barbara Gold, you look simply dreadful," I told my reflection.

I paused a moment and thought. Then I adjusted my stance to an easy swagger.

"I'm not Barbara Gold, I'm Celeste Tammany, and I do believe I need a drink. Which one of you lucky men is going to buy me a gin and tonic with extra gin?"

My voice came out brash and slightly slurred.

Perfect. Casino people always love a drunk.

Apple Bluff looked much like Cheerville. Good to its name, it stood on a bluff overlooking a meandering river, although I saw no apple orchards. Those must have been from a previous century when all this had been farmland. Now the town was a collection of middle-class neighborhoods, parks, and shopping centers. Quite dull, just like Cheerville. No doubt it had its reading clubs and topiary societies just like my town. I wondered if there was a retired secret agent here solving murder cases. It might be fun to look him or her up. Compare notes over tea.

I found the place easily enough thanks to Cynthia's directions, in a strip mall at the edge of town. These mobsters seemed to have a thing for strip malls at the edge of town. Apple Bluff's secret casino was set between Ye Olde Cheese Shoppe and Elegance Florists and Funeral Displays. All things being equal, I'd prefer the cheese, thank you.

The storefront in between had shaded windows and a modest sign saying "Apple Bluff Charity Society". A smaller sign on the door said "Members Only".

I saw all this as I drove slowly by the storefront in my bright red convertible. Rented, of course, to go with the disguise. When I rented it (still looking normal so I'd match my photo ID), the kid at the counter asked me if I knew how to drive a stick shift. I told him that every model of tank I had ever driven used a manual gear shift so I didn't see how a car would be much different. He took another look at my license after I said that. Probably searching for some small print that read, "Mental case. Do not allow to drive under any circumstances."

I found a parking spot, pulled out a little bottle of gin from my purse, and took a swig. Not so much that it would actually affect me, mind you, just enough to loosen the vocal chords and give me that lovely odor I remembered so well from the British MI6 agents in South Asia. They loved their gin, claiming it protected them from malaria. They drank the stuff like it was going out of style.

After taking a last look in the rearview mirror to make sure that awful mole was in place, I put on a saucy expression that told the world I was ready for anything, and got out.

My high heels clacked along the pavement as I sashayed to the door of the "Apple Bluff Charity Society." Or at least tried to sashay. I discovered that my sashaying days had left me and I had never noticed. Perhaps I would have found it easier to sashay without the heels, but then what would have been the point?

A middle-aged couple with a little girl of about five passed by me on the way to Ye Olde Cheese Shoppe. The girl spotted me first.

"What's that thing on her face, daddy?"

Daddy glanced in my direction.

"Hey good looking!" I called, adding a note of drunkenness to my voice.

Daddy replied with a horrified look.

His wife looked at me too, but I ignored her.

"Whatcha doin tonight, Daddy?" I called.

The wife picked up the pace, tugging along both her husband and the kid, who kept asking, "Daddy, what's that thing on her face?"

Daddy didn't respond. He just kept staring at me over his shoulder as he retreated. I blew him a kiss.

Approaching the front door of the illicit casino, I saw a security camera installed just above the front door and covering the approach. Whoever sat on the other end of that camera had seen me hitting on a married man half my age. Good. Whenever you're in disguise it's wise to establish your character early on. This guy was probably already telling his coworkers about me.

The door opened just before I got to knock.

A compact man standing about 5'10" stepped out and quickly closed the door behind him. He had pale European features, blonde hair tucked back in a pony tail, and a remarkably fit body. He moved like a fighter. This was obviously the bouncer. The last place had a bouncer too until I put a bullet in him.

That wasn't an option now. I hadn't dared bring my gun along. If they had found it, my cover would be blown and I'd be in more trouble than an eleven-round 9mm clip could save me from. Best to go incognito on some jobs.

"May I help you, madam?" he asked in a French accent.

"Oh, are you Eye-talian? I just love Eye-talians. So handsome!" I gave him a waft of boozy breath and a pinch on the cheek.

The bouncer blushed, actually blushed. I hoped he didn't have a thing for older women. That could take this mission in a direction I didn't want it to go.

"I'm French, madam."

"So exotic! Where are you from, Rome or Venice?"

To his credit, he didn't get offended. In fact, he seemed to find the whole thing amusing.

"Are you lost, madam? Are you perhaps looking for the cheese shop?"

"Cheese? I love cheese! No, I'm here to play the horses."

The bouncer tensed.

"I wouldn't know about that, madam."

I gave a conspiratorial look around me. A bored-looking shopper was walking past on the sidewalk. Then I leaned in close to the bouncer and in a whisper loud enough for the passerby to hear I said, "You know, betting on the races. This is the place! I was gonna join the casino in Cheerville but they—"

"Madam, I am sure I don't know what you mean," the bouncer said in a loud, clear voice. "This is a charitable organization for members only."

"Oh, I see." I gave him a broad wink. A couple walked by and I turned up the volume. "A 'charity' club. Very clever. Wouldn't want the cops to find out, would we?"

"Madam, I think you need to leave."

"Oh, relax, baby," I said, putting a hand on his cheek. His face, already blushing from the pinch on the cheek, turned a deeper scarlet. That must have been from embarrassment and not attraction, right?

"Madam …"

I opened up my purse to reveal a large wad of fifty dollar bills.

"Here, what's the membership fee?"

The bouncer's eyes goggled. I had taken out two thousand dollars. With his practiced eye he probably estimated the amount precisely. This was a slick outfit.

He still looked uncertain.

"Um …"

"Come on, be a sport! Like I said, I was about to join the Cheerville club. John was gonna get me in. Then it closed up! Is four hundred enough? Plus a fifty for you because you simply must be the most gorgeous doorman I've seen since the Paris Ritz."

He took the money, hesitated for a moment, and then nodded. No casino could pass up a rich drunk.

"All right. But you need to be a bit more circumspect, like me."

"Oh, are you circumcised? I didn't know Europeans did that!"

"I mean don't talk about the club!" he said, frantically opening the door and all but pushing me inside.

Just beyond the front door a short corridor led to the right before opening up into a room. The wall looked like it had been hastily added and was only there to screen the view from the outside. A few quick steps in my increasingly uncomfortable heels got me to the end of the little hallway and I stepped out into a single large room.

It looked much like the casino I shut down in Cheerville. The storefront had been converted into a gambler's paradise. Televisions fixed to every wall showed greyhound and horse races. In front of each, small clusters of men sat at tables sipping beer. They all had that hypnotized look to them I remembered from the last casino.

Scattered across the rest of the room were various roulette and blackjack tables. A row of slot machines ran the length of the back wall, except for the far corner where a door, closed at the moment, led to the back room. I suspected that like in the Cheerville casino, what had been meant as a store-room had been converted into a security center for the cameras as well as an office.

The place was pretty busy, busier than the Cheerville operation. I counted about forty people, mostly men and mostly older. It was only just past five. I supposed the after-work rush would start soon.

What struck me most about this place was how quiet it was. The televisions had the sound off since they all showed different races. The people watching them barely said a word. At the blackjack and roulette tables there was a little more conversation, but this was muted, curt, the kind of conversation you might have with someone on an elevator.

Why? Were these people ashamed, or simply so into figuring the odds that the rest of the world had disappeared?

Two employees went around the table serving drinks. Both looked like they'd do well in a fight. I also noticed the entire interior was monitored by security cameras.

"You have to fill out a membership form, madam," the bouncer said.

"No problemo, my Eye-talian friend!" I said this loudly enough that a few heads turned.

I clacked over to the nearest free seat, my ankles in agony, and sat down by a couple of men and one woman watching a horse race.

"What's your name, pretty boy?" I asked the bouncer once I was settled.

That earned me an amused look and a faint smile. "Pierre."

"Oh, I love those Eye-talian names. Bring me that form and a double martini, and get one for yourself. You must be tired after standing at the door all day. After the drink I'll give you a foot massage."

One of the men at my table choked on his drink. The other grabbed his racing form, got up, and left. The woman couldn't stop staring at my hairy mole.

Pierre scampered off. I had completely disarmed him, except for the gun he was sure to have hidden inside his jacket. I'd have to get that later.

He returned with the form, which was a simple one-pager asking for my name, address, and phone number. It also required a photo ID that they'd photocopy.

I had anticipated this, and an old connection at the CIA had whipped one up with a photo of me in disguise and a fake address. He'd delivered it by courier less than twelve hours after I sent him the picture. It's always good to have a well-funded national organization at your back.

In case you're wondering, providing retired agents with a fake driver's license for an unapproved mission is not legal. We don't always have the luxury of doing things the legal way. We're the Central Intelligence Agency, not the Girl Scouts.

At least I rented the car with my real license. Car rental agencies check licenses on the national database, you see. Illegal casinos do not.

Hopefully.

"Too bad your place in Cheerville closed," I

told Pierre when I handed him my fake license. "Got any others closer to my home?"

"No, madam."

I gave him the eye. "Pity. I would have had you request a transfer."

"I, um, need to go photocopy this," he said.

Now that he had fled and the two people remaining at my table were busy staring at the race again, I did what I came to do. I set my purse on my lap, opened it, and pulled out a racing magazine. Opening it up, I used it to cover the view of my lap from any prying eyes. I pretended to read, running my finger along the complex charts of racing statistics while my other hand slipped into my purse, pulled out a little metal box, and stuck it with a magnet on the bottom of the table.

I sent up a prayer of gratitude that the tables were made of metal. Otherwise I would have had to find somewhere else to stick it and that could have gotten complicated.

Missions are filled with these little complications. Every now and then one would get you killed.

The device was another special delivery from the agency. It picked up any cell phone conversations within a hundred meters and relayed them to a receiver which I had left in my car. Now I would be able to listen to the staff's phone conversations.

Of course I could get this place shut down right now with a simple call to 911, but that wouldn't take down the whole organization, just one tentacle. I had already seen how well these thugs compartmentalized their organization.

The transceiver stuck to the bottom of the table, well out of sight unless someone got on their hands and knees and looked for it.

Mission accomplished. I wouldn't learn any more by sitting here, but I couldn't just run off after making such a grand entrance. They'd suspect me for sure. So now I was obliged to gamble for the next couple of hours.

Pierre brought me the gin and tonic I had ordered.

"Oh, you're such a darling!" I cooed. He moved off before I could say more, like remind him that I wanted him to drink with me. It would have been nice to pump him for information.

Since I was now forced to drink and gamble, two things I've always found a bit dull, I decided I might as well make the most of it. I made a scene, roping reluctant men into conversation and pestering them to buy me drinks. I started drinking gin like an MI6 agent stuck in the jungles of Burma. After the second gin and tonic my drunken act became less of an act. Out of the corner of my eye I caught people pointing at me and laughing, and overheard snatches of unkind conversation about me, but that was all part of my plan. The best way to hide is in plain sight. Security is looking for the man or woman with shifty eyes, the one who hangs back and acts as an observer. Instead, I was the center of attention for everyone except security, who had stopped paying me any mind once the money started flowing from my purse.

And flow it did. In return for being the evening's comic relief, I got the latest "hot tips" from the hardcore gamblers on which dog or horse would win, which roulette wheel paid out more, and which slot machine was "looser". I was feeling pretty loose myself.

I followed all their advice and lost $800 in less than two hours.

This was getting to be an expensive investigation. There was no way I could ask the CIA or the Cheerville police to put illegal gambling on expenses.

After an especially big loss, when the "sure bet" greyhound I put $100 on at ten to one odds came in last, Pierre returned with two gin and tonics. I focused for a second and realized it was just one gin and tonic. The drinks were catching up to me.

"Thanks, daaaarling," I said, and placed a hand on his chest. I could feel his heart rate go up.

Just then my own heart rate went up and I suddenly felt stone cold sober.

Someone had walked into the club who I recognized.

The Exterminator.

SIX

I was sure it was him the moment I spotted him walking through the door.

I'd only seen him briefly through a car window a month ago, passing by and wearing shades, and again in my house when his face was covered by a balaclava. If he were any ordinary man I would have never been able to recognize him.

But the Exterminator was an extraordinary man. He moved with the deadly grace of a panther, and his crystal blue eyes had that dead expression of a true career violent criminal. You didn't get that look with car thieves or embezzlers, no matter how long they'd been at it. This man made his money by physically hurting other people.

Why? I'd never understood that despite all my

time in the most violent parts of the world. Some people, little people, got a sick enjoyment from the sufferings of others. They could be dangerous but they were also weak, terrified of their own suffering and thus they ended up acting as cowards. People like this man, however, did not kill for pleasure or even for money, since the money would bring them no pleasure either. That emotion had long since gutted out in their hearts, assuming they had ever felt any pleasure in the first place. People like the Exterminator killed because it was in their nature to kill. Asking them why they did it would be like asking you or I why we eat lunch.

He wasn't particularly large or well-muscled. He was fit, certainly, but it was more the fluid grace of his movements and the hard look in his eye that told me how dangerous he was. I looked him over for weapons and couldn't see any. That meant he knew how to hide them. Someone like this guy always went armed.

He stalked across the casino, heading from the front door straight for the back way. His gaze roved around the room and took in every detail. Career criminals always did that. I've seen that roving eye on every type of lowlife from crack dealers to confidence men. I suppose I had the roving eye too, but I'm one of the good guys.

His eye roved in my direction. I put an arm over one of my reluctant companions and gave a toast to something or other. My mind and my lips had long since parted ways.

Oh my. I was drunk on duty. And even worse, I shared a room with at least one and probably several trained killers.

Luckily my disguise was good enough to fool him for the moment and he didn't slow down as he went to the back door, punched a key code into the pad by the door, and stepped through. Of course he blocked the pad with his body so nobody, including little old me, could see the code.

I threw some money onto the roulette table, lost, and threw some more money down. And lost again. To kill some time, I walked (stumbled really) to a table with a good view of the back door and watched a horse race. I lost. I also didn't see anyone come out of the back.

Enough. I had gained access to the club, placed the transmitter, and gotten a good look at the Exterminator's face. Job done. It was time to go home before I really made a fool of myself.

Wobbling on those agonizing high heels, I made my way for the door.

"Stop!" a voice called behind me.

I froze. This was it. I'd gotten drunk on the job

and had made some mistake, a mistake that had blown my cover and would now cost me my life. Tensing, I slowly turned.

Pierre stood behind me. He smiled and extended a laminated card. On it was printed "Apple Bluff Charity Society" and a member number. 1016. More than a thousand people came to this place? They must be making money hand over fist!

"Thank you, gorgeous," I slurred.

"Do you need help to your car, madam?"

I almost said yes and caught myself at the last instant.

"Oh, you're such a dear. No, I'm fine. See you soon!"

"Be careful driving home, madam."

If I didn't know Pierre was a member of an organized crime syndicate, I would have thought that he actually cared. Perhaps he did in a way. I suppose he didn't want me to get pulled over for drunken driving and spill the beans about where I drank so many gin and tonics.

I chuckled as I revved up my convertible. I may have had one too many but I was an expert driver, having driven everything from Jeeps and motorcycles to Humvees. I bet in my youth I could have outdriven cute little Pierre. Outfought him too.

With my driving expertise, no one on the road would notice I'd had a few.

No one, that is, except the cops.

They pulled me over before I even got out of town.

When I saw the flashing lights in my rearview mirror, I felt a spike of fear. The alcohol washed it away. I could handle this.

I pulled over, popped a breath mint in my mouth, and waited as the cop called in my license plate number.

Then he walked up to the car. He was young, not as attractive as Pierre but certainly fit in a uniform better than Grimal.

"Hey, darling!" I said, hoping to disarm him.

"May I see your driver's license, please?"

"Here you go, gorgeous," I said, handing him the fake ID.

"Celeste Tammany," he read. "Did you rent this car, ma'am?"

"Of course!" Reality poked through the alcoholic fog. "Um, no. My dear, dear friend Barbara Gold rented it."

"Do you have permission to drive it, ma'am?"

"Of course! Barbara is unwell and I'm just doing a few little errands for her."

"Ma'am, I detect the presence of alcohol on

your breath. Would you mind stepping out of the vehicle, please?"

"Why do you people always say 'vehicle'? It's a car. Why the imprecision?"

"Just step out of the vehicle, ma'am."

I did, and just then one of my heels decided to break. Down I went, at least partway. The police officer caught me.

"What a gentleman!" I said, hugging him.

"Ma'am, sit back down. I'm going to give you a Breathalyzer."

"If you fall I will catch you I will be waiting, time after time," I sang. Cyndi Lauper. Great musician.

"Just stay there, ma'am."

He took my keys.

Things got a little fuzzy after that. I remember breathing into a tube and making the machine go off like red alert on Star Trek. He then had some questions about my driver's license, which by this time the dispatcher had told him was bogus.

I waved that little detail away like it was nothing.

"Just call Arnold Grimal. He's the police chief over in Cheerville. He'll explain everything."

"I know who he is, ma'am. Is he a friend of yours?"

"Boon companion. Bosom buddy. Comrade in arms. Well, not really."

"And what is he going to explain, ma'am?"

"That I'm on important police business, that's what!"

"I think you need to come with me, ma'am."

The next thing I remembered was being handcuffed and put in the back of the patrol car. I suppose he would call it a "patrol vehicle." I dozed for a while on the way to the station. Who knew that the backseat of a patrol vehicle could be so comfortable?

The next thing I knew I was being given my one phone call. I called Grimal.

"What do you want, Mrs. Gold?" He sounded irritated.

I lowered my voice so the policeman standing nearby couldn't hear. "I'm in a bit of trouble here in Apple Bluff. I was looking into that thing we talked about, and the police pulled me over. I'm in custody."

"What? Why? Did they bust the place?"

"No, they don't know about it. At least I don't think so. You see, I went in disguise and to get in character I had a few stiff ones at the casino and got pulled over for drunk driving."

A strange sound came over the line. It sounded

like laughter, but muffled, as if he had put his hand over the phone.

It took him a minute to reply.

"So they're charging you?"

"Yes, for that and for driving with a false license and stealing a rental car from myself."

That strange sound came from the other end again. It took longer for him to get back to me.

"Hold on, Mrs. Gold, I just got an urgent call on the other line."

"Wait! This is more important! Just explain to the …"

My voice trailed off. He was no longer there.

I waited. And waited. The policeman grew impatient.

"He's just on the other line. Give me one minute and he'll be back," I assured him.

One minute turned to two, then five. The policeman took the phone from me and hung it up.

"He can call you back," the cop told me.

The next thing I knew I was in a cell. I felt mortified. It took a long time to doze off. The bed wasn't nearly as comfortable as the back of the patrol vehicle.

SEVEN

I dreamt about witches.

The witches had long green noses covered in hairy moles. They drank gin and tonics and played roulette while cackling at me. They kept winning, and every time they won they cackled louder. It took me a minute to wake up to the fact that the cackling was real.

I opened my eyes, squinting as the harsh light of the jail cell jabbed them. My retinas felt like a pair of frying eggs.

The cackling continued.

Blinking, I focused on a couple of figures on the other side of the bars. One was the officer who arrested me.

The other was Police Chief Arnold Grimal.

Grimal was cackling like the Wicked Witch of Cheerville.

When he saw I was awake he stopped cackling and stood there rubbing his hands and grinning at me.

"Is this Mrs. Gold, sir?" the arresting officer asked.

"Oh yes! It took me a minute to see through the disguise but it sure is!" He broke off into another round of cackling.

"Is it true she was on police business? We also got a call from someone in the CIA."

Grimal's face fell. "That means a get out of jail free card, doesn't it?"

"For the false identification and the car theft charges, yes sir. But they didn't mention anything about the drunk driving."

Grimal's face lit up like a child at Christmas. He looked back at me with glee.

"So high and mighty, and here you are in a cell with the cockroaches."

"Cockroaches? Where?"

Blearily I looked around and saw a small black spot on the floor near my feet. I hate to admit it, but I flinched. I've never liked cockroaches. I'd rather have someone shooting at me.

I summoned my courage and took a closer look.

"That's not a cockroach," I said.

It was my hairy mole. It had fallen off during my sleep. I picked it up and put it in my pocket.

"Now what are you doing?" Grimal asked.

"It's a mole. Part of my disguise," I mumbled.

The arresting officer took me out of the cell, charged me, and Grimal drove me home. He hummed the whole way.

"I got too into character and the booze caught up with me," I said by way of explanation.

Grimal hummed louder.

"Stop that," I snapped, "we have an investigation to run."

"Did you find out anything besides the price of drinks?"

I was tempted to hit him. I had a sure shot right for the side of his neck. It would incapacitate him for a good five minutes, but seeing as how he was driving us at 60 miles per hour down the highway I thought better of it. I'd had enough car trouble for one day.

"I placed a transceiver so we can pick up their cell phone calls. Plus, I got a good look at the Exterminator."

Luckily for me, I remembered to grab the receiver from the rental car before getting driven home.

"We'll have a police artist sit down with you and do a sketch. Come in tomorrow once you, hee hee, sleep it off."

He dropped me off at my son's house, where I was still camping for fear of the Exterminator. All I wanted to do was roll into bed, curl up in a little ball, and die of embarrassment.

What had happened? It had been a long time since I had drunk so much. Sometimes I had to in my line of work, and while I've never been much of a drinker, I could hold my own. Four or five gin and tonics over the course of a couple of hours shouldn't have laid me low, especially considering how watery the casino made their mixed drinks.

I tried to remember the last time I had downed that many drinks. There was that party in Sonora back in 2002. I had drunk a lot more and didn't feel nearly as badly as I did now. And that had been mescal, far deadlier than gin. It was the Exterminator of alcoholic drinks.

I lay on the sofa rubbing my ankles. They screamed in pain from wearing those heels and I knew they'd be sore all day tomorrow as well. And on top of that my neck hurt, probably from sleeping in the back of the police car. Sorry, police *vehicle*. And I had a headache. And a queasy stomach. Whatever happened to that middle-aged woman who drank a Mexican Army captain under the table? He'd been in his thirties and I still bested him. And why should wearing heels for a few hours give me so much pain when I used to climb mountains and feel fine the next day?

I couldn't deny it any longer, I was getting old.

It felt unfair. Of course, every senior citizen feels aging is unfair. It takes a lifetime to get comfortable with yourself and build up your family and career to what you want it to be, and then your knees start hurting, your vision goes, and you drop off into little naps in the middle of conversations. It felt doubly unfair for me. I had always been at the peak of health. Field operatives had to be. But now here I was at the not particularly advanced age of 70 with all these minor physical problems. And I knew they would only get worse.

I have to say it took me by surprise. "Sure," I told myself, "other people will be going downhill at 70, but not me. I exercise, eat right, don't smoke or take drugs, and drink in moderation."

Except for the occasional mescal and gin bender. All in the line of duty, of course.

The sad fact is, living a healthy lifestyle isn't always enough. How well you age is as much related to genes as to lifestyle. Also, while every couch potato is guaranteed to end up with some serious health issues later in life, the kind of rugged living I had enjoyed for so many years had obviously taken an equal toll. All that crouching behind cover while waiting to ambush an enemy had done a number on my knees. All those harsh days in deserts and mountains had probably given me that little spot of skin cancer they removed from my forearm a couple of years ago. Lugging eighty-pound packs on countless forced marches had certainly contributed to the back pain I now enjoyed.

I hadn't been a junk food gobbling television watcher, but I had swung to the other extreme, and now I was paying for it.

I poured myself a tall glass of tomato juice. It's the perfect hangover cure. Alcohol drains vitamins A and C from your system and tomatoes are rich in both. A good thing to remember if you ever have to infiltrate an illegal casino.

Sitting down with my tomato juice, I turned on the cell phone receiver. It's a clever little device that looks like a tablet with a speaker attached. The touchscreen shows all the calls being made at the moment and you touch on its number to listen. It also records all the calls into a two terabyte hard drive and logs the time for each call and the number of the cell phone it connects to.

Work was the last thing I wanted to do right

now but I had a mission to accomplish. I turned on the receiver and saw five cell phones currently in use within the transceiver's coverage area. I touched the first one.

"And on your next delivery could you bring an extra two kilos of gouda? Someone made a big purchase and I'm getting low."

Must be the manager of Ye Olde Cheese Shoppe. I put that number in the discard folder so it wouldn't show up on the screen again and clicked the next number.

"Yeah honey, I'm still at the office. Work has really piled up. I'll be back when I can."

A gambler making his excuses. I felt tempted to call the number he was calling—his wife's, no doubt —and tell her what he was really up to. Hangovers always make me grumpy.

I was a good girl and didn't wreck a marriage. Instead I put that number in the discard folder along with the cheese merchant's.

" … Marlboro Golds, and pick up some more gin while you're at it. That lush nearly drank us dry."

Lush? Who are you calling a lush? I was getting into character!

The next time I go I'll have to be a little less in character. But if I got lucky, there wouldn't be a next time. If they talked enough on the phone, I could gather all the evidence I wanted from the safety and comfort of home.

Sadly, that was the last bit of conversation. The call ended. I put both numbers in the priority folder.

The other two numbers were uninteresting calls from the gamblers, one by a guy telling his boss he felt ill and had worked from home all day, the other from a woman calling her son to wish him a happy birthday and that she'd be late for his party because she was "stuck in traffic".

I rolled my eyes, a habit I'd picked up from my grandson Martin. I'd never rolled my eyes until I had a teenager in my life. Now I found myself rolling my eyes regularly. Perhaps I should stop chasing criminals. It would give me less reason to roll my eyes.

For a while there were no more calls. Then I wasted some more time listening to gamblers giving excuses for not being wherever it was they were supposed to be, heard all about some rude customer who had just left the cheese shop, and even overheard a call from Elegance Florists and Funeral Displays about how roses shouldn't be sent to a particular funeral because the deceased had been allergic to them. Why would that matter?

I had to wait another hour before the same number that asked for cigarettes and gin called a new number. My ears perked up. They unperked when all I heard was a routine call about picking up the money that evening. Of course he didn't reveal where the money went, since that was known to both parties, but I still learned the pickup time and got a third number for the priority folder.

That was enough for one night. I could skim through the recordings tomorrow and spend the rest of the day listening to any new calls. My son's guest bedroom was calling to me.

The next morning I woke late to a pounding headache, neck ache, back ache, and ankle ache. I might have had some more aches but those four aches were achy enough to drown out all other aches.

After a hangover special of bacon and eggs and black coffee, plus more tomato juice, I checked the cell phone receiver. It took me most of the morning to scan through the calls and I came up with nothing interesting except a couple of first names and two more numbers to put on the priority list. Investigative work can be slow sometimes, especially when the targets were careful like these fellows. They took care never to use last names or talk about specific places. I heard several references to "the boss" but "the boss" never seemed to call anyone. Smart. Cell phones were easily overheard. No doubt they were adding another level of security by using "burners", cheap disposable cell phones. You could buy them with cash and fill them up with credit you also bought with cash, making them untraceable. They were favored by drug dealers and other criminal types. I kept listening, though, slowly creating a profile of their work habits and first names.

Slow going. I hoped I'd get something juicy soon. My son and his family came back in a few days. The Exterminator needed to be in jail or exterminated before then.

Just as I was finishing up the previous night's recordings, Octavian called me.

"Hey, pretty lady. Want to bet on some horses today?"

"Um, not today, Octavian. I'm not feeling well."

"Oh no! The *doro wat* not agree with you?"

"What? Oh, the wat, I mean the *doro wat*. No, that was tasty. I think I might be coming down with something."

"That's too bad. Maybe tomorrow?"

"Maybe. I think I'll take a nap now."

"Oh, all right."

Octavian sounded disappointed. He was going

to get even more disappointed when the Apple Bluff casino got shut down like the last one.

Instead of the nap that I really did feel like having, I went to see Grimal. He'd brought in a police artist who sat with me for an hour until he'd made a good likeness.

Grimal took a look at it when it was done.

"Looks clear enough, but weren't there two of them?" he asked.

"Excuse me?"

He waggled two fingers in front of my eyes and grinned. "You know, double vision?"

"Very funny. Run this through the system."

I left before he came out with any more witticisms. I decided to listen to the receiver for a little while longer, take a well-earned nap, and then catch up on anything recorded while I was asleep.

One of the priority numbers was engaged to an unknown number. I clicked it, and the first words I heard made my blood run cold.

"The target's boyfriend is here. Shall we take him?"

EIGHT

I rang Octavian's number, desperately hoping that statement hadn't meant what I thought it did.

I nearly fainted when he picked up and I saw mine and his numbers appear on the receiver.

"Hello, pretty lady, are you feeling better?"

"Octavian! You're at the casino in Apple Bluff."

"No I'm--, um, how did you know?"

"You have to get out of there. You're in danger!"

"Oh come now, why would I be in danger? Cynthia knew somebody and set it all up. It's safe. Come on down."

"Don't ask me how I know, but you need to get out of there right away and find the nearest policeman."

"Policeman?"

"Listen. Just trust me on this. You need to get out of there right now."

"Huh? You're not making any sense. Hold on, one of the workers is coming over."

"Octavian!"

I heard him talking to someone, his words too faint to make out. He had obviously taken the phone away from his head. I heard something that might have been "come with us". Then I heard Octavian shout, "Cheating! You're crazy." There came a thud, and the phone hung up.

I immediately called Grimal, telling him to send a couple of plainclothesman as backup. He wanted to go in guns blazing, desperate to repeat his hero routine, but I talked him out of it. We needed to do this carefully in order to keep Octavian from getting hurt. Plus, I was still hoping to nab the whole gang and put a stop to this once and for all.

As I rushed to get changed into my disguise, I listened to the cell phone scanner.

"We got him. Pretended to kick him out for cheating and then brought him around back," said the voice that had ordered cigarettes.

"You still have him on the property?" asked a suave voice I didn't recognize from a number I hadn't seen before. Could this be the boss?

"Yeah, but in the back. The marks don't suspect a thing. We're keeping him quiet."

When they said "marks", that meant the gamblers. They didn't see them as people, only targets from whom to get money. They wouldn't look at Octavian as a person either. They only saw him as a way to get to me.

They'd been watching us more closely than I suspected. How much else did they know about me?

"Pump him for information, but don't get rough. We don't want him making noise. Just scare the hell out of him," the suave voice ordered.

Cigarette man gave a harsh laugh. "Oh, he's plenty scared already!"

He hung up. As I finished my disguise and drove as fast as I dared for Apple Bluff, I didn't hear any more calls from the gangsters. Not a single one. Their silence made me more afraid than their words.

As I pulled into Apple Bluff, I got a call from Grimal.

"We're in luck. There was a drug crimes unit monitoring some alleged dealing near a school. We got them reassigned. Officers Lichtmann and Budge. They're in a gray sedan parked in front of the cheese shop."

Grimal sounded all business. Despite his many

faults, when the chips were down he could be relied upon. Sort of.

"What's your plan?" he asked.

Plan? I didn't really have a plan.

"I have a membership card. I can get in with no trouble. They're holding him in the back room so get one of your men to cover that exit, but keep out of sight of the cameras. There's sure to be one at both entrances. I'm going to try and extract Octavian without any gunplay. If I need backup, I'll call you."

"I'll be there in ten minutes," Grimal said. "A patrol car will be just around the corner waiting to move in if needed."

"Good. Thanks." I hung up and focused on driving. My heart was beating dangerously fast. My doctor had warned me about stress, saying a woman my age should take it easy. That had been a civilian doctor who didn't know me or my past. Take it easy? Avoid stress? That didn't seem to be the life I was fated to live, even after retirement.

Grimal called me a few minutes later as I was getting off the highway to tell me that an off-duty officer who happened to be near the strip mall and was out of uniform had been called in and was monitoring the back entrance. That made me feel better. Grimal also said he was on the way. That didn't make me feel anything at all.

I parked well away from the view of the camera in front of the door. I was back to driving my own car and I didn't want them to notice the change. I got out, wearing flats and a more sensible dress this time, but with the full disguise on. The only addition to the ensemble was my handy 9mm automatic tucked in my purse. I had even brought along my spare clip. Despite my assurances to the Cheerville police chief, I had my doubts about getting out of this without gunplay. In fact, I was pretty tempted to go in there shooting every mobster I saw.

As I walked across the parking lot, I could feel myself breaking out in a cold sweat. I took several slow, deep breaths, forcing myself to calm down.

Scoping out the parking lot, I spotted the two drug cops sitting in their car. One was on his cell phone while the other pretended to read a newspaper. The parking spaces near the entrance to the casino were mostly full. Good, the mobsters hadn't shut the place down. It was business as usual while they kept my boyfriend hostage in the back room.

Another spike of fear shot through me, forcing me to take several more slow breaths. What if that suave voice I had heard on the phone had been the

Exterminator and not the head of this operation? What would he do to poor old Octavian?

I needed to calm down and get in there.

I stopped by the front door and focused. I'd faced a lot worse situations before, and fear would not help me, only a clear head could. I recalled a time when James was trapped in a burning building in Palestine while a platoon of jihadists took potshots at him from outside. The area around the building had been completely open, just a fallow field. If he had fled the building he would have been a dead man. If he had stayed in the building he would have been a dead man.

Octavian was in no worse situation. I had gotten James out of that building, and I would get Octavian out of this one.

I cleared my head, got into character, and rang the buzzer.

Pierre didn't answer this time. Instead it was another mobster, one of the ones who had been serving drinks the day before. I forced myself to smile.

"Hello darling, remember me? I'm back for more fun!"

"May I see your membership card, madam?"

I felt like sticking my gun in his mouth. Instead I handed over the card.

"Welcome back. Glad to see you so soon."

"Any good action this morning?" I asked.

He kept a good poker face. "No, pretty quiet so far. It will liven up now that you're here."

"It sure will," I muttered.

I entered the casino and found the bouncer had been correct, it was pretty quiet. About a dozen people were there, mostly watching the races. A desultory poker game was going on at one of the tables. If it had been any other situation I would have found the place boring. I wondered what all the other cars in the parking lot were for. Perhaps a big sale of extra stinky Limburger at Ye Olde Cheese Shoppe? An especially popular corpse at Elegance Florists and Funeral Displays? Who knew?

I took a seat by myself near one of the televisions at a table to the side of the room so I could keep an eye on both entrances. It was out of character for me to sit alone, so to compensate I ordered a double whiskey on the rocks. I couldn't bear to even think about gin.

My mind raced. Now what? I had come here with only a vague plan of extracting Octavian from this mess, but I had no idea how.

We seemed to have the advantage. Police guarded both entrances, I was inside, and the mobsters had no idea they were in danger. The problem was, I didn't have direct communication with the police and since the cop at the back had been off duty, he probably didn't have a radio to contact the cops at the front. Communication is vital in an operation like this, and we had none.

Come to think of it, was the off-duty officer even armed?

I took out my racing form and pretended to study it, all the while trying to keep an eye on the thugs who ran this place. They appeared remarkably calm, as if kidnapping a kind seventy-year-old man was a daily occurrence for them. Perhaps it was. They certainly didn't seem to expect any trouble.

My phone buzzed. Grimal. Picking up, I could hear he was in his car.

"What is it?" I asked, trying to keep my voice calm and level.

"I'm almost there," he said.

"Well, that makes me feel better. Any news?"

"None. We're keeping watch," Grimal was using a cocky, overly manly tone I didn't like. It would have sounded convincing coming from the Exterminator or Pierre or even Octavian, but Grimal? Not so much.

"Nothing much going on here either," I said, keeping my voice low.

"Once we get into position we'll give them a few minutes to come out. If they don't, we'll have to announce ourselves and demand they give up."

"Are you crazy?" I hissed. "You know how that could turn out."

"What choice do we have?"

I noticed one of the waiters passed close by and gave me a look. I realized I wasn't in character. I took a slug of whiskey and my stomach roiled. Gorge rose in my throat and I forced it back down. Oh dear, the last thing I needed while trying to rescue my new boyfriend was to get sick.

Waiting until the waiter was out of earshot, I whispered, "Look, you just stay put. If you interfere, I swear to God I'll nail you to the wall. Let me handle this."

"How?" Grimal's question came out as a challenge.

I didn't have an answer to that. I needed a bit of time to assess the situation. Maybe I'd see an opening.

"Just sit tight and don't do anything foolish."

I hung up on him, then texted him.

Text me if there's any news. Can't risk another call.

Just then a waiter came up.

"Are you ready to place a bet, ma'am?"

"Um, yes." Putting away my phone. Had he seen? His face was a mask.

I placed a bet on an upcoming dog race, picking a dog at random.

Time stretched out. I resisted the urge to glance at my watch.

The race started. As subtly as I could, I glanced around the room. Nothing seemed amiss.

Why was I so nervous? I'd been through worse than this more times than I could count. This shouldn't be bothering me at all. Was it because I was getting on in years? No, I'd solved two murders and been in a gunfight since moving to Cheerville and none of that put me so out of sorts. What had changed?

Octavian.

Every time I'd been on a mission before, I'd either been alone or with someone qualified to handle the job. I'd always worried when James was in the line of fire, but I knew he had the skills to get himself out of it. Octavian didn't. The only thing he'd ever shot was a deer. He'd never had to deal with a situation like this. The poor fellow might be so afraid he'd get a heart attack.

The waiter's voice behind me snapped me out of my unpleasant thoughts.

"Here are your winnings, ma'am."

I admit I jumped a bit. I hadn't been this edgy on a job in years. My training kicked in, however, and by the time I turned to him I was the drunk, happy floozy Celeste Tammany.

"Oh, thank you darling!" I said, my gaze flicking to the television for the first time since the race had started. The race had ended and a new one had begun without my noticing.

The waiter handed me $300. I blinked. That could buy a lot of *doro wat*.

My phone buzzed. A text from Grimal. I waited for the waiter to leave and read it.

A man matching your description of the Exterminator is about to come through the front door.

Wonderful. This day just got worse.

NINE

A moment later my would-be assassin entered the casino. Like the last time, his roving eye took in everything in a few seconds. I forced myself not to look at him, instead pretending to read the racing journal. I even had my eyes follow the lines of type although my mind didn't register the words. Someone with the Exterminator's level of training would notice a little detail like someone staring at a paper but not reading it.

Thus I didn't see how long he looked at me. That he looked at me for at least a moment I had no doubt. That man missed nothing, and his gaze rested on every single person in that room in the time it took him to cross it and get to the back door.

As he punched in the key code, I saw my chance.

A ridiculously dangerous chance, but one I couldn't miss.

To cover my movements as I stood up, I made a show of pulling out my cell phone and dialing a number.

What they didn't know was that it was the number of the police chief of Cheerville. I needed him to hear this.

He picked up on the first ring. "Grimal here."

"Be quiet and listen," I murmured, tucking the phone in my breast pocket and hoping he'd be able to hear everything.

It only took ten steps to get behind the Exterminator just as he was opening the door.

He noticed me after five steps and automatically began to close the door with himself still on my side.

He stopped doing that when he spotted the 9mm in my hand, shielded from view from the rest of the room by my large purse.

Men always wonder why women carry large purses. More than one has told me, "It looks like you have half your possessions in there."

A gun takes up space, fellows, and a lady needs her makeup and various other things too. Plus, a large purse can be used as a club, a distraction flung in an opponent's face, and it can hide the fact that you're carrying a gun.

I made sure the Exterminator saw, though.

He reacted as I suspected he would. He stopped closing the door, obeying the implicit instructions given by the dark circle of the gun barrel moving towards him. He glanced to the left and right, hoping someone else saw this. When he realized he was alone in this situation, he looked at my face …

… and looked right through my disguise.

Nothing like pointing a gun at someone to give your game away.

His eyes narrowed. It wasn't hatred or malice or even a threat, it was a hard focus, a ruthless determination that assured me that if I didn't play this exactly right, I'd be a dead woman very, very soon.

All this happened in the last five steps that brought me close enough to him that he had no chance of dodging or getting away, but just out of reach of any punch or kick he might try. I was not at all confident that I could fire before he could disarm me.

"Go through that door," I said in a low voice.

He turned, and with no sudden moves that might make a gun-wielding grandma jumpy, opened the door the rest of the way and stepped through it.

I followed him.

I didn't have much time. One of the thugs in the front room was sure to have seen me go in with him and they'd be coming. Plus, there were the thugs in the back room.

The thugs in the back room were three in number. One sat in front of a row of camera monitors and was just in the act of standing up when he saw my gun, hesitated for a second, and sat back down with his hands in the air.

The other two were Pierre and a man I didn't recognize, flanking a chair on which Octavian sat. He looked more confused than nervous.

He didn't have a mark on him. Lucky for the bad guys.

"Celeste!" Pierre shouted. "I mean, Ms. Tammany. What are you doing?"

"Shut up," I said in a harsh whisper.

I closed the door behind me and motioned with my gun for the Exterminator to take a couple of more steps away from me and the others to move away from Octavian. They behaved like little lambs, or wolves in sheep's clothing.

Once they were a safe distance away from me

and my boyfriend, I said in a loud, clear voice, "Grimal, can you hear me?"

"Yes." His voice sounded muffled and small inside my pocket. I preferred him that way.

"I'm in the back room of the casino and I have Octavian. I also have three hostages. I'm going to—"

I cut off as I heard the electronic lock beep behind me. Someone had just punched in the code.

The door started to open and I yanked it shut.

The man on the other side hadn't expected resistance and let the doorknob slip through his fingers. Next time he'd have a better grip on it and there was no way I would win a tug of war with a man half my age. Twenty years ago, yes, but not now.

I had all of three seconds to get out of here.

"We're coming out the back," I said, half to Grimal and half to Octavian.

"And there are cops surrounding this place so don't try anything," I went on.

That was for the mobsters' benefit.

I grabbed Octavian by the lapel and tugged on him. He stood and followed me. A quick glance told me there were no other threats here. The back room had little but for a desk, a safe, and a rack of shelves filled with snacks and liquor bottles. The back door stood only a few yards away. My four prisoners had just happened to position themselves between me and it.

"One side!" I barked.

Just then several things happened at once.

First, the door to the casino opened as I thought it would.

Second, a crash and a shout in the main room told me the mobsters had more trouble than little old me.

Third, the Exterminator dove for the ground and rolled.

Fourth, a bag of potato chips hit me in the face.

I never got to see who threw the potato chips. Whoever did it really should have thrown a bottle, but no doubt he threw the first thing he could grab from that supply shelf. It was more to distract me than to hurt me.

It worked.

During the second I was blinded I fired at my feet, hoping to hit the Exterminator.

The bag of potato chips fell away and was replaced in my vision by something far worse—the Exterminator rising up, hands reaching for me.

Like I suspected, the Exterminator had dodged my blind shot.

Then Octavian did something that warmed my

heart. He punched the Exterminator right in the side of the head.

It didn't do a thing, of course. I'm not sure the Exterminator even realized he'd been punched, but Octavian had shown what a sweetheart he was in any case.

Then I had other things to worry about. I felt a vice go around my gun hand and an irresistible force move my aim away from my opponent. I let off another round in any case, just to give Grimal extra warning that things had gone south. One shot might not be enough for that fellow. He could be a bit slow on the uptake.

I hissed in pain and let my gun drop to the floor. It was a choice between that and having my wrist broken. I take my daily calcium supplement, but I couldn't rely on that to save me from a man of his strength.

Octavian punched him again, just as a brave and protective boyfriend should. This time the Exterminator did notice, and gave him a slap with his free hand that sent poor Octavian tumbling.

The muzzle of a gun pressed against the back of my head. It has a very distinct feeling, most unpleasant. You can't mistake it for any other object being pressed against your skull. I've felt it before and I had hoped I would never feel it again. It was one thing I was looking forward to in my retirement.

"Don't move," said the owner of the gun, no doubt the gentleman who had just come through the door. I heard a shout and a crash in the main casino room before he slammed the door shut.

"Be careful with that gun, young man," I said in a voice loud enough for Grimal to hear. "There are policemen outside who won't be very happy if you shoot a senior citizen."

"Well then I guess we'll just have to use you as a hostage, won't we?" the Exterminator said. He gave me a quick pat down, found my phone, turned it off, and tossed it to the side. He also found the pepper spray in my purse and pocketed it.

I looked him in the eye. It wasn't an easy thing to do.

"You know how hostage situations always end," I told him, rubbing my wrist. "There is no bag of money and no free ride to the airport at the end of the rainbow. You're cooped up in here—" a gunshot outside interrupted me "—and you're not getting out. They won't let you get away, not for the sake of little old me."

The Exterminator gave me a disturbing little smile. It felt more unsettling than when he had been lunging for me.

"A normal civilian, no, but a CIA agent?" he said.

My heart did a little flutter.

"How could you know that unless you … oh. Oh, dear."

He gave a smug nod.

"CIA?" Octavian called from the floor. "What's going on here?"

I looked down at Octavian sprawled at our feet and felt more than a little surprise. Poor fellow. The shock of having learned that I was up against a rogue CIA agent had made me forget he was down there.

"If this doesn't work out, Octavian, I want you to know that I'm quite fond of you. In the meantime, I think it would be best if you kept quiet. You're in over your head."

He struggled to his feet as the Exterminator shoved past us and opened the door to the casino a crack.

"Hey, cop! We have two prisoners back here, the old CIA lady and her boyfriend."

"You hurt her and you'll be in a world of trouble," Grimal's voice growled from the main room. "We got the rest of your gang in custody. Give yourself up and no one gets hurt."

I rolled my eyes just like my grandson did. I

knew Grimal would jump the gun, hungry for glory.

"That's not how it's going to play," the Exterminator replied. "Me and the boys back here are walking out with these two old people and you're going to let us."

"What about the guys out front?" Pierre asked him. "Get the cops to let them go."

The Exterminator's reply told Pierre just where the "guys out front" could go. It was most colorful.

"Don't swear in front of a lady, young man," Octavian said with a frown as he picked himself up from the floor.

I put a hand on his arm. "Now's not the time for chivalry."

The Exterminator fired a shot out the door. From the angle I could tell he didn't intend to hit anyone, just get attention. The gamblers all gasped and screamed anyway. People with no training scare easily.

So did Police Chief Grimal.

"There are innocent people here!" he shouted, his voice coming out an octave too high.

"And none of them will get hurt if you do as you're told," the Exterminator said. "Call off the guys at the back. We're going to drive out of here. I'm sure you've called the police helicopter over in

Farmington. That's the closest one. It can't get here for at least ten minutes. We'll be well away by then but if we see it, we shoot the prisoners. If we see you following us, we shoot the prisoners. If you don't call off the cops at the back right this instant, we shoot the prisoners. It's your move, flatfoot."

Grimal didn't answer.

TEN

I've never liked the sound of Grimal's voice, which sounds bossy and weak at the same time, but the long silence that came after the Exterminator's demands made me yearn to hear it again.

At last he spoke.

"How do I know you'll release them?" Grimal asked.

I rolled my eyes again. What a dumb question.

"Who said anything about releasing them?" the Exterminator asked. "I'll kill them if you don't do as I say. I'll release them later if you and they behave, and if I feel like it."

"If you hurt her, you'll fry," Grimal said in what was supposed to be his tough guy voice.

"If I get caught I'll fry anyway."

"For illegal gambling and kidnapping? No you won't."

I felt like strangling that man. Just how slow on the uptake could he be?

The Exterminator laughed.

"No, for all the other stuff I've done. You got five seconds to call off the cops. Put it through the radio loud enough that I can hear you."

Grimal swore under his breath, and then said in a loud voice, "All units move back. I repeat, all units move back. We have a hostage situation. They're moving out the back door and getting into a vehicle. Do not intercept or follow. I repeat, do not intercept or follow."

I hoped the local cops would listen to him. He was probably the most senior officer on the scene, but he wasn't actually their police chief. Plus, I suspected that the police in Apple Bluff were just as inexperienced as the police in Cheerville. Most likely, this was the most serious crime any of them had ever faced. I prayed none of them would do something stupid.

I glanced at Octavian to see how he was holding up. To his credit, he looked remarkably well. He was pale and sweating of course, and his eyes were as wide as saucers, but he didn't look like he had boarded the Heart Attack Express.

That was a relief. If he keeled over because of the stress, I would never forgive myself.

At a curt command from the Exterminator, Pierre checked the camera monitors, then went to the back door and peeked out.

"Looks like the coast is clear," he said.

"All right," the Exterminator said to him. "You and Jack take the old man and go out first. Al, Constantine, and I will come next with the prize catch."

Pierre glanced at me. I wasn't sure how to read his expression. He'd masked his features, but his eyes showed a mixture doubt and … something else.

He only looked at me a moment. The guy named Jack drew a gun, took Octavian by the arm, and went to join Pierre.

I held my breath as they went out to the back lot, half sure that some jumpy small town cop would fire at them.

No one did. A moment later the Exterminator tugged me by the arm, his pistol ready to air out my brain. He led me out to the back lot, where a little to the right of the door the thug named Jack was pushing Octavian into the back door of a black Humvee with tinted windows. Pierre gave a nervous look around and jumped in the driver's seat.

No cops were in sight. I strained my ears for the sound of the police helicopter but didn't hear it.

They put me in the back seat next to Octavian. The Exterminator and two of the others sat in the middle seat, watching us. Pierre started the engine and drove at a moderate speed around the building to the front.

He was a professional one; all of them were. The impulse for a normal person would have been to slam on the gas and peel out of the parking lot. That might have made the cops jumpy, though, so Pierre played it cool. None of the others panicked either. They were tense, ready, but none of them looked afraid.

As we got to the front parking lot I could see the mess Grimal had made of this. As I suspected from the sounds in the front room, he had blustered in. Now the gamblers and the mobsters were all lined up in front of Ye Olde Cheese Shoppe, their hands on their heads. Grimal obviously couldn't tell a career criminal from a bored suburban gambler. I guess he planned to press charges against the customers to set an example. In reality, the only example he had set was how to turn a hostage situation into a double hostage situation. It would have been more appropriate if he had lined everyone up in front of Elegance Florists and Funeral Displays.

We might be needing their services before the day was out.

The prisoners looked odd having no policeman to guard them. As instructed, the officers had pulled back to the far end of the parking lot. I saw three patrol cars, a total of six uniformed cops and Grimal, all with their service pistols trained on the Humvee.

Pierre slowed the vehicle.

"Shall we pick up the guys?" he asked.

"We don't have room for them all in the Hummer," the Exterminator said.

I could see Pierre's face in the rearview mirror. He did not look happy.

Nevertheless, he sped up and got onto street.

"Now what?" he asked.

"Plan C," was all the Exterminator said.

I allowed myself a slight smile of satisfaction. Apparently we had thrown a big enough spanner in their works that Plan A and Plan B were no good anymore.

"What's going on?" Octavian asked me. "You're CIA?"

"Quiet," one of the thugs barked.

Yes, Octavian, quiet. Not only did I have to figure a way out of this mess, I had to figure out how the Exterminator knew my CIA connections.

So who was this Exterminator fellow? Ex-CIA, apparently, and one who somehow still had access to the database. That wasn't an easy thing to do. The CIA database is the Holy Grail of computer hackers worldwide. Anyone who can break in can sell that information to governments with very, very deep pockets.

He didn't strike me as a hacker, though, and he certainly wasn't still on the payroll. So he must have a partner inside the organization who had warned him about me.

Wait, not necessarily. Despite his speed and strength, he was not a young man. He was in his late thirties at least, perhaps mid-forties if he looked younger than his age. That meant that if he had joined right out of college like so many of our recruits, he had overlapped with my time of service for ten or fifteen years.

Did he know me?

I wracked my memory, trying to place him, but came up with a blank. I had never worked with the Exterminator before, and as far as I could recall I had never met him.

Of course, I would have been more visible to him more than he to me, because I had been a senior operative while he would have been a junior recruit. Perhaps I had been pointed out to him, or he had attended one of my lectures. James and I had given a few over the years on special operations and Middle Eastern politics. Although they had been for CIA employees only, some of the crowds had been pretty large. He could have easily been there, and he seemed like the kind of guy who would never forget a face.

He must have flipped when he recognized me at the casino in Cheerville. No wonder he made a tight U-turn and sped off. He needed time to think about the implications.

His caution had saved my life. If I had been anyone else, he would have gunned me down on the spot.

So he had seen me speak in his early years with the CIA and then at some point he had gone rogue. I was amazed that he remained alive and in the United States. Few operatives went rogue, and when they did they usually either disappeared into remote parts of the world or they got the protection of hostile governments in exchange for information. Even so, we managed to liquidate most of them in the end. Going rogue was a very risky business, and to do so and remain in the U.S. was doubly so.

There had to be a major incentive. I doubted these small-town casinos brought in enough money to pay his salary, so what else was going on?

It looked like I had bit onto the little toe of one giant of an operation.

I glanced at Octavian, who couldn't stop staring at me. He wasn't even staring at my hairy mole anymore. Instead he searched my eyes, looking for reassurance or an explanation or something, anything that would make all of this make some sense.

Poor man, I'd dragged him in way over his head.

Way over mine too. How was I going to get out of this?

For the moment, there wasn't a thing I could do. Even without Octavian as an additional risk, trying to get a gun from one of these thugs and sticking them all up was a suicidal proposition. I had no choice but to sit tight and see what Plan C entailed.

For the moment all it entailed was a quick drive away from the outskirts of Apple Bluff and down one of the many winding, two-lane country roads that crisscrossed the region. Trees closed in on both sides. The occasional house flashed by. Pierre turned on a police scanner and we heard the chatter.

" … E.T.A. five minutes," came a voice almost drowned out by the sound of helicopter rotors.

"Stay out of sight and we'll advise," came

Grimal's voice. He sounded so panicked his voice had risen to a falsetto.

"Don't worry, I got them in my sights and I won't lose them," came another voice.

"Keep back!" Grimal shouted.

Everyone looked out the back window. The unmarked car that had been staking out the casino was a good distance behind us, disappearing on the curves and reappearing on the straightaways. Pierre slowed down and put on his hazards.

"Suspects' vehicle is slowing. Looks like they're going to make a break through the woods."

The unmarked car was closing in on us now. I wanted to wave my hands in warning and scream, but with the Humvee's tinted windows they would neither see nor hear me.

What they saw instead was the Exterminator roll down the window and open up with my very own 9mm. He knew they'd do ballistics on the rounds fired, and he didn't want to compromise his own weapon. Illegal firearms, as his no doubt was, didn't come cheap. A true professional. Even in a firefight he thought clearly.

Thankfully he thought clearly enough not to add a double police homicide to his long list of crimes. Instead he landed two rounds in the radiator, and as the car swerved, took out the left front

tire. That made the car swerve in the other direction before going off the road, thumping up a low
rise, and slamming into a tree.

I gritted my teeth. Were they okay? A turn in
the road kept me from knowing.

I glanced at Octavian. He was keeping his cool.
Unlike most civilians, he didn't panic or shout
angrily at the Exterminator for shooting at a pair of
police officers, instead he sat very still, looking very
pale. I put a hand on his.

"I'll get us out of this," I said.

He gave me a look that showed he did not have
much confidence in that statement. I have to admit
I agreed with him.

The police scanner crackled to life.

"Pursuit vehicle reporting. We've been hit," a
pained voice said. "They spotted us and took out a
tire. We had a crash."

"You guys okay?" someone asked.

"Brian's all right. I slammed my wrist against
the steering wheel. I think it's broken. Car's totaled.
We've lost them."

Grimal's voice cut in. "We've called for backup.
We'll cordon off the entire area."

"Of course you will. It won't matter, though,"
the Exterminator said with a chuckle.

For the next fifteen minutes, Pierre took a

looping path along several back roads until I was thoroughly disoriented. The police scanner continued to crackle out commands and information. The Cheerville police and several other police stations had been called in to help. They got busy cordoning off the area. Their task was helped by the fact that the river was on our right and the police had already blocked off both the bridges. Every now and then I saw a gleam of water through the trees.

I have to admit the police were showing speed and professionalism. Even Grimal displayed more than his usual lackluster ability, and yet our kidnappers didn't seem worried at all. The only thing that seemed to bother them was the possibility of the helicopter moving in. They kept looking out the window and up.

At last Pierre drove the Humvee onto a little-used dirt track through the woods. He drove only just far enough to get out of sight of the road, then parked and turned off the engine.

We all got out. With Pierre leading, and the Exterminator right behind me and Octavian and covering us with my own gun, we marched down the track for about a hundred yards before coming to an abandoned farm. A dilapidated house stood to one side and a barn stood directly in front of us.

I'd spotted several of these farms in the region, relics of a more rural time before the city workers and retirees moved in. Most had been torn down and turned into modern homes or apartment complexes, but some still survived. Just a few yards beyond flowed the river. Pierre led us to the barn. I could just see on the other side of it a concrete ramp leading down to the water. The ramp was covered with an awning. Oddly, the awning continued a few yards into the water, supported by metal poles.

"You're going to take us on a boat?" I asked, surprised. "That's even more visible than your Humvee."

One of the thugs laughed. "Oh, it's better than a boat. You'll see."

Pierre unlocked a padlock securing a heavy chain and slid the barn door open. We stood at the entrance for a moment as our eyes adjusted to the relative darkness within.

Once I could see, my jaw dropped almost to the floor.

A pickup truck had been backed into the barn and hitched to the back of it was a long trailer.

On top of the trailer was a miniature submarine.

This was getting weird.

ELEVEN

"Who are you people?" Octavian gasped.

"A very well funded crime syndicate with a rogue CIA agent as their enforcer," I replied. That much was obvious, and it wasn't like they were going to tell him anything more.

Now I realized why there was a tarpaulin extending some distance into the water. They could enter the river without being seen from the air.

The Exterminator clapped his hands and rubbed them together with obvious relish.

"Okay, boys. This is our ticket out of here. The sub only seats six and there are seven of us. It's going to get pretty cozy in there."

"Why don't we ditch the old man?" the thug

named Constantine said. "We don't need him anymore."

My heart fluttered. The way he said it made me know what would happen to my boyfriend. I glanced around the barn. A wrench lay on the ground not far off. I might just be able to get to it. As I said before, I was still up for one good hit.

But there were five of them.

"We take him," the Exterminator said to my immense relief. Then he gave me a cold look. "Because as long as her friend is alive our little old CIA agent here won't cause any trouble, will she?"

I nodded.

Of course I would cause trouble as soon as I was able, and the Exterminator knew it, but he also knew that I wouldn't risk Octavian's life, which seriously narrowed my options.

This is why evil so often defeats good. Evil isn't limited by conscience.

Pierre got into the pickup truck while the others started clambering onto the submarine. One opened the hatch in the little conning tower and went inside. The one named Al motioned with his gun for us to follow him.

Octavian slumped, putting his hands in his pockets. Then I was surprised to see him perk up. He treated me to a smile.

"If we don't make it out of here alive, I want you to know something," he said.

"What's that?" I said, moving closer to him.

"That fake mole is hideous."

He chuckled. Actually chuckled. Was the fear making him giddy?

"Move it," Al ordered.

Octavian clambered up onto the submarine and with the help of one of the others managed to get into the hatch and disappear inside.

Just as I moved to follow him, Pierre called out from the pickup truck.

"I don't think it looks hideous at all. It makes you distinct."

I raised an eyebrow. "Didn't you hear it was fake?"

Pierre looked disappointed. I didn't want to think about why. I had enough to contend with here.

Hauling myself onto the submarine, I gave it a quick assessment. This sort of technology wasn't my forte, not much use for subs in the Middle East, but I could tell it was a recent model. I spotted sonar, some radio gear for when it was on the surface, and a periscope with both optical and CCTV capabilities. It looked like it ran on diesel.

Once inside, I squeezed past a couple of seats to

take my place beside Octavian in the second-to-last row of seats. The Exterminator and Al sat in the very back, their guns at the ready.

"We don't have enough seats," Al told me. "You're going to have to sit on the old fart's lap."

"I am not an old fart!" Octavian objected.

"You better not be," Al shot back. "If you let one off in here I'll shoot you."

"Crude boy," Octavian muttered.

"Don't make trouble," I said, sitting on his lap. Octavian put his hands around my waist and suddenly remembered himself. He pulled them away, hesitated, and finally rested them at his sides.

"Don't worry," Octavian whispered. "I'll get us out of here."

Yes, Octavian, you go right ahead and believe that.

Everyone else crowded in, the last man leaving the hatch open. I heard Pierre start up the engine to the pickup truck, the vibrations making the whole submarine tremble.

"It's like Magic Fingers," Octavian said with a chuckle. "Remember Magic Fingers?"

"What are Magic Fingers?" Al asked.

"Before your time," Octavian said. "They had them in motel rooms. You put a quarter into a slot and the bed would shake. Very soothing."

"Why, you dirty old man!" Al laughed.

"I am neither dirty nor old."

Al snorted.

I turned to look at Octavian. He was acting strangely. I hoped the stress wouldn't make him crack. He looked at me, smiled, and flushed. I realized suddenly that I was sitting on a man's lap, something I hadn't done in far too long, and I kept squirming.

Well, at least Octavian's last moments would be pleasurable.

The pickup backed up and we went down the ramp. We all tilted back, which made me lean against Octavian. He didn't object.

Pierre stopped the pickup, switched off the engine, and we hard him clomping around on top of the sub, his footsteps sounding loud and metallic inside the narrow confines of the submarine. There were several loud snaps as he released the clamps and then we felt ourselves sliding backwards.

The minisub plunged into the water, bobbing along like a cork. I craned my neck to look up out of the hatch and saw we were still under the tarp. Even if the helicopter was nearby, we wouldn't be spotted.

Then the interior dimmed as Pierre's body filled the hatch. He squeezed inside, pulled the hatch closed and locked it. Then he clambered into the pilot's seat.

"You can drive just about anything, can't you?" I said.

Pierre gave me a grin over his shoulder.

"It's a pity such a talented young man is wasting his life with these hooligans," I went on.

Pierre's look turned doubtful and guarded.

"Just get us out of here before the heat tracks us down," Constantine said.

Pierre started the engine. It was well maintained and purred like a tiger. When he switched on the CCTV, we could see on a screen right above his head the interior of the barn. I kind of hoped to see Grimal burst in at the head of a SWAT team, but no such luck. The barn slowly receded and raised up as Pierre backed up the sub and began to submerge.

Within another moment we were under, and the CCTV went black.

Then it went a muddy brown as Pierre turned on a light at the front of the sub. Dimly I could make out the bottom, but the water was so murky I could barely see ten feet.

Luckily the sub also had sonar, and when Pierre switched it on I saw an excellent 3D image of the area around us for a good hundred yards. The riverbed sloped away behind us, Pierre still backing up and submerging. The sonar was so sensitive I could even see the poles that held up the tarp until we receded out of range and they disappeared.

Pierre turned the sub and we headed upriver, skimming over the top of the riverbed at a depth, the readout told me, of ten yards. Another readout told me we were going 30 mph. A pretty good speed for such a small sub. This was almost military grade.

"You're running drugs, aren't you?" I asked. "There are cheaper ways to get away from the police, but this is the perfect thing to bring drugs up the river from the port. Heroin, perhaps? It's been flooding the market recently."

No one replied. That told me all I needed to know. Organized crime had been getting more high tech in recent years. In England, drones had been used to fly drugs and weapons into prison. A remote-controlled Cessna filled with cocaine crashed in Florida, no doubt bound for some secret drop off point. Cybercriminals had become so good that the only way the governments of the world had found to control them was to put them on the payroll with lavish salaries. A gang using a minia-ture submarine to transport hard drugs along the nation's rivers wasn't much of a stretch.

"It's stuffy in here," Octavian said.

He was right. The air felt close.

"That's because we're overloaded. We shouldn't have brought you along," Constantine said.

"I'll turn up the oxygen levels," Pierre said, reaching for a dial. "What the hell? The oxygen tanks are almost empty. Al, I told you to fill them last night!"

"I did!" Al objected.

"No you didn't, or they'd be full," Pierre shot back.

"You idiot!" the Exterminator shouted, smacking him upside the head. Al cringed, even though he held a gun in his hand.

"Do we have enough to make it?" the criminal named Jack asked. He wasn't much of a talker, but he sure asked what we were all wondering.

"Not even close," Pierre replied.

Octavian and I traded glances. He took my hand and squeezed it.

TWELVE

"What do we do?" Al said, rubbing the side of his head and looking fearfully at the Exterminator.

"Let's ditch the old man," Constantine said. "We can throw Al overboard too."

"We're not ditching anybody," the Exterminator said.

I decided not to remind him that he had ditched several of his colleagues back at the casino.

"It wouldn't do any good anyway," Pierre said. "The tanks are almost spent. We'll have to surface."

"They'll see us," the Exterminator said.

"We'll just surface enough to put of the periscope and air tube. We won't be all that visible. Besides, they won't be looking in the middle of the river anyway."

The Exterminator gave a grunt that expressed that he didn't like the idea but that there wasn't much he could do about it, and if the cops cornered them, he'd shoot Al. Quite an expressive grunt, really. He and Grimal should have a grunting contest.

Al understood the significance of the grunt too. He looked like he was going to be seasick.

I didn't feel too well, either. The air was getting stifling and I found myself taking great gulps just to fill my lungs.

The depth readout indicated we were surfacing, although I didn't feel the motion. Pierre switched off the front lights as the camera showed us break the surface, or to be accurate the camera on the top of the periscope broke the surface. The front of the sub appeared as a dark shadow in the water in front of it. I wondered how visible it would be from the police helicopter.

Pierre flipped another switch and a little circle of sunlight appeared on the back of the seat in front of me. A breeze came through a little pipe on the roof, sucked in through an electric pump.

"Excuse me," Octavian said, shifting under me and plopping me on the seat. He leaned forward and got right under the pipe, his face turned upwards. I had a grand view of his derriere a few inches in front of my face. Not a bad derriere considering his years. Must be all that Seniors' Yoga.

"What are you doing?" Al demanded.

"Getting some air. I feel faint."

"You're blocking it from the rest of us!" Al shouted.

"We wouldn't be in this mess if you had done your duty, young man."

"I'm warning you—" Al's warning got cut off by another smack upside the head courtesy of the Exterminator.

"Catch your breath and sit down, old man," the Exterminator said.

Octavian remained where he was for another few seconds and then got back in our seat. I sat back in his lap.

"Feeling better?" I asked, concerned.

Octavian treated me to a grin. "Splendid."

We continued up the river in silence for several minutes. The periscope showed the river ahead. I couldn't get a very good view of the sky and didn't see any sign of the helicopter. Once a barge approached and Pierre closed up the air pipe and dove for a few minutes until we were past it. The air turned foul almost instantly. Within a couple of minutes, we were all panting and sweating. Al got lots of nasty looks. As soon as we surfaced again, Octavian complained of faintness and put himself under the air pipe until he caught his breath. Pierre dove again when we came to a bridge, and once again Octavian had to catch his breath right below the pipe when we surfaced.

After the bridge, we came to a long stretch of the river where there was no traffic except for a couple of distant speedboats. Then Pierre slowed and turned. I saw a small tributary ahead. He pulled into it and we continued for a couple of minutes before coming to a large mansion by the riverbank. A private marina stood in front of it with a speedboat and a yacht. As I expected, there was also a dock covered by a tarp that extended over the water. A low wall shielded it from view of the river. We could surface there without being seen.

Pierre expertly steered the sub into the dock, surfaced, and switched off the engine. From the camera display of the periscope I saw a young man run into view, take a quick look around, and tie a mooring cable from the pier onto the prow of the sub. Pierre hadn't radioed in, probably thinking it best to keep radio silence now that there was a manhunt on. This fellow had obviously been expecting them or at least had been assigned to keep watch.

Pierre opened the hatch and one by one we all climbed out. I took a big breath of fresh air and looked around me. I stood on a dock in a small, private marina. On the hill nearby was a white-washed mansion, so bright in the sun that it hurt my eyes after the half-light inside the submarine. There were several large picture windows on the ground floor but the glass was all tinted and I could see nothing inside. Nevertheless, I had no doubt that our arrival was being watched.

My trained eye took a quick scan of the property. The hill was bare of everything but grass. A few stumps showed that until recently, some large oaks had stood there but had been cut down, obviously to afford a better view of all approaches to the house. The woods started a good fifty yards from the house, and were hemmed in by a chain link fence. Discreet cameras attached to the roof of the house covered every angle.

"It looks like we've made it to the lion's den," Octavian said, standing beside me with his hands in his pockets. He looked remarkably unconcerned.

"You don't have to put on a brave face for me, I'm scared too," I told him.

"But you're a secret agent."

"That doesn't mean I don't get scared when I'm on the job."

"You'll have to tell me more about your work once we're away from bad company."

I gave him a peck on the cheek. "You're a dear."

"Yuck, old people kissing," Al said.

This time it was Pierre's turn to smack him upside the head.

"What was that for?" Al said, rubbing his head again.

"For being rude to your elders," Pierre said.

Pierre wound up and slammed a punch full in Al's face. The gangster flew backwards and landed on his back.

"And that was forgetting to fill the damn air tanks!"

"Enough," the young dock attendant said. "The boss wants to see you all inside. You wouldn't believe the manhunt they're putting on for you. They've called in cops from half a dozen towns! Whoever these old codgers are, the cops sure care about them."

Grimal, care about me? More likely he saw his precious career about to go down in flames if anything happened to me on his watch. Still, it felt nice to be the center of attention.

Before we left the cover of the awning, the dock attendant stepped onto the lawn and took a good look around. Signaling that the coast was clear, the rest of us followed. We were hustled along by our captors, who obviously didn't want to be caught in the open.

"You should give up, fellows," Octavian said, sounding out of breath as we ascended the hill. "It will go easier on you."

"Shut up," the Exterminator said. "You're only alive because Barbara here cares about you."

"There are worse reasons to be alive than that," Octavian panted.

As we got to the colonnaded front porch, the door opened and yet another tough looking young man stood there. This was turning out to be a big operation.

They led us through a marble front hall and past a sweeping grand staircase to a large living room.

An elderly man in a silk dressing gown greeted us. Right away I could tell this was "the boss". He was only a few years younger than Octavian and I, but he had a presence about him. He stood erect, a large brandy snifter in his hand, and his sizeable belly and receding hairline did nothing to take away from his aura of command.

The thugs who had kidnapped us all changed their body language when they got in the presence of their master. Even the Exterminator looked a bit less cold and arrogant, although more out of respect than any sort of subservience.

The boss twirled his brandy snifter and stuck his nose inside the glass. He seemed in no hurry to start the conversation. He took a deep breath of the brandy fumes and then a little sip. Despite his relaxed attire, on his wrist he wore a huge gold and diamond Rolex that probably cost more than most people's annual salaries. The decor in the room was similarly flashy. Lots of mismatched antiques and garish Italian furniture. Nineteenth century paintings of fox hunts hung on the walls

Cocking his head, the boss studied me for a moment and said, "So this is the great Barbara Gold. I've heard so much about you, and you have caused me no shortage of trouble."

It was that same suave voice I had heard over the cell phone scanner.

"You'll be in a lot more trouble if you don't let us go right now," Octavian said.

The boss barely glanced at him. "Do keep quiet, Mr. Perry. You are only here on sufferance."

"And why am I here?" I asked.

"Because you make an excellent bargaining chip, Mrs. Gold. My casino operations have been far too compromised to continue with that particular branch of my business, but I might be able to continue with other operations unmolested. I think we can come to an understanding."

"I don't think so," I replied.

The boss motioned towards Octavian with his brandy snifter.

"Take him away and put him somewhere secure. Mr. Black, you stay here with us. Your insights into CIA operations will be most helpful."

This last bit was addressed to the Exterminator. I had never heard him referred to by name before. No doubt "Mr. Black" was as fake a name as it sounded.

The others led Octavian away. As he left the room he called back, "Don't worry, Barbara, they'll find us."

The boss smiled as the door closed. "A brave man you have there. Good for me he isn't as resourceful as you dear departed husband James."

I glared at him. "Don't mention his name again."

The boss merely shrugged and gestured to a pair of plush armchairs. I took one and the Exterminator took another. He still had my 9mm in his hand and still had it trained on me. I took this as a sign of respect. Not that I appreciated it. I would have preferred that he underestimated me like everyone else. The boss reclined on a leather backed sofa and took another sip of brandy.

"That is a truly unattractive costume, although I must say most convincing."

"So I've been told. Can we get to the point, please?"

The boss chuckled. "Certainly. Mr. Black here still has connections with members of the Central Intelligence Agency who are, shall we say, more flexible in their thinking than your typical member of government service."

"You mean corruptible."

"If you want to put it that way, yes. Now the CIA has a certain *esprit de corps*. They do not want to see one of their retired agents die a gruesome, horrible death, and they are willing to compromise on certain things. They've made bargains before, and for you I am sure they will make bargains again."

I leaned back in my chair and let out a long, slow breath. Being in the foreign branch all my career I was used to compromising with ideals for the sake of the greater good, but that had been in rough and tumble parts of the world where civilized rules didn't apply. But here in America? I didn't want to think we were compromising on such things here.

Like everyone else I'd heard the rumors. Dirty tricks in elections. Drug running. Wrecking the image of public figures hostile to the Agency. Of course it would all be rationalized on the altar of "the greater good", but that was a darn slippery slope when your goals were anything less than over-throwing a bloodthirsty dictatorship.

"So what are you proposing?" I asked. No, I wasn't interested in making a deal, not for my own life, not even for Octavian's life, but I wanted to feel them out. If I got out of this, any information they let slip could be highly valuable.

The boss took another sip of his brandy, kicked off his slippers, and reclined on the sofa.

"In exchange for you and Mr. Perry being released unharmed, and an immediate and perma-nent cessation of all casino operations, your agency agrees to not investigate our other operations or share information about us with any other govern-ment agencies for five years."

"So you can keep running heroin up the river with your sub."

"We will not go into details, Mrs. Gold, but as you have no doubt figured out by now, we have a varied and wide ranging business. The casino network was only the newest branch, although I must say it was spreading quickly. We will shut all the casinos down, and there are quite a few. We will also give you the names and addresses of two spies within American industry who have been selling technical data to Russian companies. Mr. Black here can arrange it with his people inside the CIA, as long as he has your consent."

"What's the other option?"

"The other option is unprofitable for both of us. You've seen too much, so you and Mr. Perry will have to die. The CIA will discover this sooner rather than later, and come after us with a vengeance. We are a resourceful enough operation to survive, but will will take a severe financial loss and no doubt some of our lower-raked members will be killed or caught. I'd prefer to avoid that, as I am sure you would prefer to avoid spending all of eternity with Mr. Perry in an unmarked grave."

"You put forth a convincing case. How would this work?"

The boss got a gleam in his eye. He thought he had me hooked. I pegged him for a greedy, cynical man who assumed everyone else was equally corruptible. The Exterminator showed no reaction at all. He would be harder to convince.

But I didn't really intend on convincing them. I was stalling for time, hoping they'd make a slip. I'd already scoped out the room and had noticed a lovely Chinese vase sitting on a side table within easy reach of me. It was one of the only tasteful objects in the room and would be handy to throw at someone's head. That could prove useful. Plus, I wanted to hear more.

So I let them lay out the plan. As a show of goodwill, and no doubt as a further temptation for me, they would let Octavian go immediately. He would serve as message bearer. Then a secure channel between me and the CIA would be opened, and the Exterminator would work his back channels. Once an initial agreement was set up, the gangsters would release the name of one of the industrial spies. Then, when the CIA's side of the bargain had been completed to the gangsters' satisfaction, they would release the second name as well as yours truly. As security, the Exterminator will have already disappeared to a place not even known by his boss. If the CIA broke their side of the bargain, the Exterminator would hunt me down, and kill Octavian in the bargain too.

I made a good show of looking reluctant but tempted. That kept them going. When you don't have many options, it's always good to stall for time. It gives you a chance to gather more intelligence and perhaps a new option falls in your lap.

After fifteen minutes of haggling over details, one did.

"This is the police," a megaphone blared outside. "We have you surrounded. Release the hostages and come out with your hands above your heads."

How did they get here?

I didn't have time to ponder that. It was my cue to throw the Chinese vase at the Exterminator's head.

THIRTEEN

The vase landed on the side of the Exterminator's head with a satisfying crash. He had instinctively looked towards the nearest window and thus didn't see the vase coming.

I was up on my feet in an instant, or what passed for an instant these days, and leapt across the room to where the Exterminator lay on the floor. Okay, I walked quickly, quickly enough to get to the gun before the boss could. That fellow was obviously the brains of the operation and not the muscle. All he had managed to do was throw his brandy snifter at me, miss, and get to his feet.

I leveled my gun at him. It felt good to hold it in my hands again.

"Stop right there. It's over!" I shouted.

A door opening behind me told me that my assessment of the situation had been overly optimistic.

I spun around and pumped a bullet in the gut of the first thug who entered. It turned out to be the fellow named Al. That was fine. He had nearly made us suffocate in that submarine. No one would mourn his loss, least of all me.

The man behind him ducked back out of sight so quickly I didn't get to see who he was. I crouched behind the chair for cover and turned to the boss, only to find him disappearing through a side door. I fired a round after him to send him on his way.

I didn't get a chance to see if I hit him or not because the next moment a spray of bullets raked the room. It came from a submachine gun from the sound of it.

Crawling behind the couch as bits of wood and shreds of fabric flew everywhere, I waited until I heard a click of an empty magazine, then popped up, ready to take the machine gunner out, but he'd already gotten back behind the doorway again.

I had two or three seconds while he changed magazines. I leapt to my feet and sprinted for the door …

… or at least I tried to. My knees, unaccustomed to crawling, screamed in protest and I felt a sharp twinge in my lower back, no doubt from that cramped ride in the submarine. I staggered a couple of steps, and only just managed to level my pistol in time for him to appear again.

Thankfully my reflexes were better shape than my joints, and I put one through his forehead. His submachine gun clattered to the floor.

I got against the wall so as to be out of sight of anyone else coming through that door and edged to the submachine gun where it lay just inside the room. It was an Agram 2000, a Croatian model that you don't see much of outside of Eastern Europe. It has a 32 round clip that only an idiot could miss with (said idiot now lying dead on the floor) and a clever ergonomic design that included indentations for each finger on the main grip. In front of the magazine was a loop with a thumb-hole grip you could use to steady the gun with your other hand as you set off a long burst. The perfect compact submachine gun for the discerning lady of a certain age.

I glanced around the doorway, leading with my pistol. No one else was in the front hall. Scattered gunfire throughout the house told me they were otherwise occupied. I discarded my pistol, not having anywhere to put it, and scooped up the Agram 2000.

Now I was ready to hunt.

My heart told me to look for Octavian, but my brains and instinct told me to go after the boss. I had no idea where they had taken Octavian, but if I could get the boss then I'd have a good bargaining chip. I closed the door through which the attackers had come and moved over to the side door. I listened, didn't hear anything, and then flung the door open, immediately ducking back out of sight in case the boss was lurking on the other side waiting to shred me with a shotgun or something.

That happened to a colleague of mine once in El Salvador, but that's another story.

A narrow hallway dead-ended after ten feet with a door to the front and another to the right. The one to the right almost certainly led back to the main entrance room, so I choice the door in front of me.

I tried it and found it locked. A short burst from my Agram 2000 took care of that.

My, what a kick in that little thing! I had forgotten just how much a submachine gun tries to buck and jump in your hand like an unbroken horse in those Westerns James always used to watch. Submachine guns are made for indoor and urban fighting and need to be compact, but making them compact sacrifices a lot of accuracy. Good thing I had that ergonomic grip or I might have shot up every part of the door except the lock.

But seeing as I did have it, I was rewarded by the door springing open. The boss, still in his silk nightgown, was just descending down a hatch in the floor of a small library and study, a briefcase in one hand and a .45 revolver in the other. He took an unaimed shot at me that didn't come close to hitting me but made me shrink back enough that I didn't get a chance to return fire.

Then he was gone. The hatch had carpeting on it and when shut would be invisible to the casual eye. A secret door down to … something.

Submarines, hidden doors … what next, a death ray? This guy had obviously read too many spy novels.

I edged up to the hatch, angled my gun over it, and without exposing any other part of my body, sent a burst down the hatch. I couldn't hear anything above the belch of the gun. Back in the Seventies they used to call submachine guns "burp guns" because when you fired them they sounded like a 300 pound trucker getting rid of the gas from his latest six pack. Once I stopped firing I stood silently for half a minute and heard nothing. Either I had killed him or he was alive and well and waiting for me.

Best to assume the second. Being a pessimist is a healthy worldview in my line of work.

I waited a few seconds, the sounds of firing rising to a crescendo in the house around me. The thud of a shock grenade echoed through the building. It sounded like the police had launched a full scale assault. They had obviously stopped caring about me and Octavian. That meant the gangsters had forced their hand by trying to make a break for it, guns blazing.

And what about Octavian? My heart trembled to think of him in the midst of all that.

I pushed that thought aside. I had work to do.

I sent another burst down the hatch and then peeked over. A metal spiral staircase, now riddled by my bullets, descended into near darkness. I peered down as well as I could and all I could see was a high-ceilinged cellar piled with crates. I did not see the boss but there were a dozen good places where he could hide and get an excellent shot at the exposed staircase as I came down.

I hesitated. Going down those stairs would be suicide.

Then the distant revving of an engine told me that he wasn't covering the stairs, he was making a run for it.

I hustled down the staircase as fast as I could

and saw an open door at the far end of the cellar. Daylight streamed in. Hoping no one else was lurking in the cellar, I hurried over to the door and saw it opened out onto a path leading downhill to a second dock, one around on the other side of the hill from where we had come with the sub. The boss was just pulling out in a small speedboat. A policeman lay by the dock, clutching his side where he had been shot.

The dock was about two hundred yards away, and the boat had already made it a further fifty yards and was picking up speed, turning its side to me as it moved down the tributary towards the main river.

No other police officer was in sight. Obviously the rest were busy storming the house. I heard the sound of the approaching helicopter, but once they got here the boss would be far enough away that they might mistake him for regular river traffic and not a fugitive. The police in these parts were really that dumb.

It was all up to me.

Hitting a quickly moving target at 250 yards with a submachine gun is a pretty tall order. The weapon was made for close fighting. This shot required a rifle which I did not have. And I only had half a magazine left. Enough for two decent bursts.

I aimed, as much as you can with such a short weapon, and let off a burst. The boss ducked as my bullets spat up water all around him, but he did not fall.

I took a deep breath, aimed again, and as I exhaled emptied the magazine.

Sparks flew all along the metal hull of the boat. Then one smacked into the engine. There was a brief flare of light, a cough from the engine, and a trail of smoke.

My submachine gun clicked. I was out of ammunition.

Then the boss's gas tank exploded.

A lovely ball of flame enveloped the boat, rising into the air. The boss leapt off the boat, his silk dressing gown on fire.

He landed in the water with a splash. The boat's momentum pushed it several yards away from him before it turned and capsized, still flaming.

The boss splashed frantically in the water.

"I surrender!" he shouted.

"I kind of figured that!" I shouted back.

His head went under, then appeared again like a cork, although not a very buoyant cork. So I suppose he didn't come back up like a cork at all. More like a drowning man gasping his last breath of air. His arms splashed every which way. He sputtered for a second and then shouted to me, "I can't swim!"

"If you can't swim, you should have set up your headquarters in the desert instead of along a river!"

Then I turned and went inside. I needed to find some more ammunition. I was beginning to love this little gun and I wanted to play with it a bit more.

I retraced my steps and ended up back in the living room. There I froze. The Exterminator was gone. I'd only knocked him out for a few minutes. That was bad news.

Peeking through the door, I saw no one in the front hall, just the two bodies I'd left by the door.

Just as I was leaning over to check if the fellow I'd taken the Agram 2000 from had any more ammunition, a panicked gangster ran down the stairs, in such a hurry to get someplace he didn't notice me until I got a bead on him.

"Drop that pistol!" I shouted.

He looked at me, looked at the submachine gun, and looked at me again.

"Last chance!" I shouted with as much confidence as I could muster. If he called my bluff, I was done for.

His gun dropped to the floor with a clatter and he raised his hands above his head.

"Go out the front door and surrender," I ordered.

He edged to the front door, opened it, and was rewarded by a bullet whizzing by his head.

"I can't go out there! The cops are too trigger happy!"

"Well, you can't stay in here. Move it."

He waved his hands through the door to show he wasn't armed, and then peeked out.

"Come out with your hands up!" Grimal shouted through a megaphone.

"That's what I'm trying to do!" the gangster shouted, then cautiously stepped out the door.

Once he was gone I bent over and searched the bodies, coming up with another 32 round clip.

Perfect. Once I snapped it into place I felt much better. There was still scattered firing around the house. The focus seemed to have shifted to the far wing of the building, so that's where I headed.

My knees still ached, my back still ached, my wrist still ached from where the Exterminator grabbed it a couple of hours before, and my shoulders were beginning to ache from firing this wonderful burp gun, but I ignored all those things. I could take a hot bath with a glass of wine and a painkiller later. Right now I had a man to save and several others to defeat.

Moving past the grand staircase, I came to a long hallway spattered with bloodstains but no bodies. The house had suddenly gone silent. That worried me. Usually when the police stormed a building they came in with overwhelming force screaming at the top of their lungs. This attack seemed to be a patchwork affair, disorganized and undermanned. Only one officer had been guarding the side entrance to the other pier, Grimal was still outside, no one was in the front hall or stairs or wing that I had just left, and no one was here either. Who was running this show?

Oh wait, Grimal. Silly question.

"It's just you and me, my darling little Agram 2000," I whispered. "I'm going to name you Burpette."

A chorus of shouts up ahead told me where the party was. I headed through a door and came upon the backs of several police officers. None of them saw me. If I had been a gangster, I could have gunned them all down. Between all those broad, stupid shoulders I could just make out what they were all training their guns at.

And my heart went cold.

The Exterminator held Octavian in a headlock

and had a pistol pressed against his head. He edged away towards a door.

"Let him go!" one of the cops demanded.

"If you make a move, the old fart gets it!" the Exterminator shouted back.

The Exterminator passed through the door, dragging Octavian with him.

"If I see any one of you on the way to the pier, I kill him!" he shouted, then kicked the door closed.

FOURTEEN

I had to work fast. The police might do something stupid and get Octavian killed. Plus, to get to the pier, the Exterminator would have to go around the front of the house, where Grimal was still lurking. I laid even higher odds on that fool doing something stupid.

I slipped out of the room the way I had come as the police got ready to storm the door through which the Exterminator had just disappeared. They never knew I was there.

Moving as fast as I could, I hurried back through the main front hall and out the front door ...

... only to have a bullet crack the doorframe inches from my feet.

I did a little dance and shouted, "It's me, you idiot!"

Grimal was lying prone on the front lawn, huddled behind a bulletproof riot shield. When he saw me, his eyes went wide.

"Oh, sorry!"

"Good thing you're a bad shot!" I shouted.

"Yeah, good thing!" agreed the gangster I had forced to surrender. He sat with his hands cuffed behind his back a few yards away from my least favorite police chief.

"One of the gangsters has Octavian," I told Grimal as I came down the steps. "He's headed for the pier. Call off your goon squad before they get him killed."

Grimal hesitated.

"Now!" I shouted.

I think I actually pointed my submachine gun at him, but I can't vouch for that. If I did, it was entirely subconscious. I had no intention of actually using it. Fantasies, perhaps, but no intention. Really.

Whether it was the tone of my voice or the prospect of getting burped on by a burpgun fired by a woman with a hairy mole, Grimal grabbed his radio and shouted, "Do not intercept the suspect with the hostage!"

Why do police always use the term "suspect"? Hadn't we gone beyond the suspect stage at this point? I suppose they were told in the police academy that they couldn't label someone a criminal until after they'd been convicted in a court of law.

Just then the ruthless killer rounded the corner of the house. My mistake, the "suspect" rounded the corner of the house, allegedly trying to make an escape from his alleged crimes while allegedly holding a gun to Octavian's head. Pierre, another "suspect", came just behind them.

They spotted us and paused. The Exterminator's trigger finger tensed.

"Wait!" I shouted, dropped my beloved Agram 2000. "I surrender. Take me instead. Just let him go."

The Exterminator cocked his head.

"All right, you got a deal. Move over here and do it slow."

I did as I was told.

"Slowly," Octavian said.

"Huh?" the Exterminator replied.

"'Move over here and do it slowly,'" Octavian said. "If you knew how to speak proper English maybe you could have gotten an honest job."

"Shut up or I'll shoot you."

"I was kind of hoping you'd do that so that the police officer over there could shoot you," Octavian admitted.

"Very gallant," the Exterminator said, shoving him away. "Now beat it, I got a better hostage now."

Octavian tried to get between us but the Exterminator aimed at his head and Octavian slowly stepped aside. I continued to walk forward.

I had almost made it to him, my hands raised in the air. The Exterminator gave me a nasty grin.

Just then his head exploded.

The rogue CIA agent fell onto the grass with a thud, stone dead. Pierre stood behind him, a gun in his hand and his eyes bugging.

For a moment nobody moved, then slowly Pierre bent down and placed the gun on the ground, raising his hands over his head as he straightened up.

I blinked and gaped at him, utterly confused. "Pierre … why?"

He gazed back at me with love and devotion in his eyes. "Why? Do you really have to ask why? He was going to hurt you. I'd rather go to jail for life than let anything happen to you."

Oh. Oh dear. Um, I didn't really have a response to that.

Grimal saved me from having to think of one by hustling up and handcuffing him. As the cuffs went on, Pierre looked at Octavian.

"Take good care of her."

"I will, young man," Octavian replied.

Luckily Octavian was a gambler and able to maintain a poker face.

As Grimal led him away to the other prisoner, Pierre called over his shoulder, "I'll never forget you, Celeste!"

Octavian looked at me. "Celeste?"

"An alias. Necessary for undercover work."

The old sweetie looked baffled. "But didn't he hear your real name?"

I struck a pose, tweaked my hairy mole, and said in the slurred voice of a habitual drunk, "Well, I guess he just prefers me this way. Can you be a darling and pour me a drink?"

Octavian shook his head. "I think I could use one myself."

The police came out with the last few gangsters, laying them out on the grass and frisking them. The helicopter circled low overhead, late to the party.

Grimal strutted over to us. He looked inordinately pleased with himself.

"Only two men wounded and the entire gang

rounded up. Not a bad day's work," he said with a pride that was as overbearing as it was unearned.

"Where's the Apple Bluff police chief?" I asked. "Shouldn't he be in charge here?"

Grimal gave me a grin. "He's up in the state capital for a meeting, so the honor went to me."

Unbelievable. He was going to get another medal and more headlines out of this. I, of course, would get none of the glory and all the sore joints. I was curious about one thing, however.

"How did you find us?" I asked.

Grimal nodded to Octavian.

"Mr. Perry's panic button," the Cheerville police chief said.

"His what?" I asked, turning to Octavian.

He gave me a proud smile and from his pocket he pulled out a little plastic box. With his thumb he flipped open the front to reveal a small red button.

"It's for emergencies. It calls 911 in case you've fallen and can't get up. Since you might not be able to speak, it has a geolocator on it so the emergency services can come and get you. You're supposed to wear it around your neck but that looks ridiculous so I keep it in my pocket. Those gangsters never frisked me like they did you, thinking I was just a harmless old man. Young people always underestimate us. Even my own daughter does. She bought this panic button for me. I don't need the fool thing, I'm as healthy as a man half my age, but I carry it around just to placate her. She'll never stop laughing when I tell her how useful it turned out to be."

"Mr. Perry hit that button several times during your captivity," Grimal said. "It allowed us to trace your path from the abandoned farm all the way to this place."

I looked at Octavian with renewed admiration. "So that's why you kept putting your hands in your pockets!"

He flashed me that winning grin. "That's right. I hit it before we got on the sub, and then each time we surfaced for air. That's why I got right under the air pipe. I was hoping the signal would make it out."

"It did," Grimal said. "It was faint, but it did."

"Plus I turned the volume as low as it could go and put my hand over the gizmo's little speaker so no one could hear emergency services trying to speak with me. When I didn't respond, they tracked me. Plus, I knew they'd notice there was an APB out for me as a missing person. That brought the police right here. Pretty good thinking, eh? I could have been one of those secret operatives too."

"I suppose you could have," I admitted, and smiled.

He examined my hairy mole. "All things considered, I'm glad I chose to be a stock broker. I never had to wear any nasty disguises or get shot at. Imagine dying looking like that! It doesn't bear thinking about. Hopefully we won't be having any more of these little adventures."

"I have to warn you; dating a CIA agent, even an ex-CIA agent, isn't easy."

"Yes, I've noticed, but I like you no matter what," Octavian said, taking my hand.

I felt a little squishy feeling in my chest. I gave him a kiss on the lips.

He had certainly earned it.

THE NEXT DAY found me back where it all started —in front of my mirror putting on makeup. This time Dandelion was behaving. No bolting away from intruders, no climbing up my leg and ruining my pantyhose, instead she was playing with a toy I'd made for her. It's amazing how fascinating a tennis ball on the end of a string tied to a doorknob can be for a cat. I could hear the regular *thump thump thump* as she batted it and it hit the door. It reminded me of my grandson. He was always thumping around too.

They'd be back home later that day, to find their plants watered and everything as it should be. They wouldn't know a thing about what had happened. Grimal had kept my name out of the newspapers. His name, of course, was in all the headlines.

That annoyed me more than I care to say. At least he didn't put up a fuss when I stole the Agram 2000. It was more useful in my hands than in some evidence locker. My darling little Burpette now sat next to my 9mm in the drawer of my bedside table, ready to greet the next bloodthirsty assassin who decided to make an appearance.

Standing in front of the mirror, I put on way too much powder and the brightest shade of lipstick I had been able to find. Then I added the mole.

Yes, I was going as Celeste Tammany. I had an appointment to visit Pierre in prison. The poor dear had asked for me. It seemed only fair, after what he did for us, that I give him some sympathy before his long prison term. Hopefully his sentence won't be too long. I'd heard that his lawyers were trying to convince the prosecutor to be lenient in exchange for his testimony against the others in the gang.

I looked at my creation in the mirror. Truly

horrid. Why the young man found this attractive was beyond me, but there's no accounting for taste.

After watching Pierre pine for me through the glass at the prison visitor center, I had a lunch date with Octavian. I had a few things to explain, to say the least. He was being a good sport about all this. Discovering in your golden years that you're dating a former CIA agent who solves the occasional murder and has a predilection for getting into gunfights must be a bit hard to absorb.

He had invited me to Bangkok Fire, a Thai restaurant with a reputation for five-alarm five specials that was in, of all places, Apple Bluff. I think Octavian was trying to reassert his manhood after all the gunplay and kidnappings and whatnot.

What a darling. I would have to remember to take off my disguise before meeting him. He'd been through enough already.

Then I remembered what he had said to me after the Exterminator went down: "I like you no matter what."

Hmmm, perhaps we should test that?

Yes. I'll take the disguise off but leave the hairy mole on. We'll see what he thinks of that.

I did warn him that dating a CIA agent wasn't easy.

ABOUT THE AUTHOR

Harper Lin is the *USA TODAY* bestselling author of 6 cozy mystery series including *The Patisserie Mysteries* and *The Cape Bay Cafe Mysteries*.

When she's not reading or writing mysteries, she loves going to yoga classes, hiking, and hanging out with her family and friends.

www.HarperLin.com